## Death of a Rising Star . . .

"Looks like you've been pretty busy, Jessica," Elizabeth said as she picked up a magazine off of Jessica's bed.

"I'm just trying to find one good reason why Julia Reynolds would commit suicide, especially since everything was going so well for her."

"I doubt you'll get any real answers from a magazine. It's hard to know what to believe."

"The gossip papers say that Julia had a history of depression, and that's why she did it. But I have my own theory. I think it was all a big accident. Julia jumped off that building at the wrong time, it's as simple as that."

"Or maybe the movie studio is keeping the whole thing under wraps," Elizabeth said. "Think about it—if you just signed on a huge movie star and she died because of some stupid mistake, the whole company could go down."

"Yeah, New Vision could lose millions over this," Jessica agreed.

Clearly, the idea of suicide just didn't seem to fit. In the high-stakes world of Hollywood, there was one possibility that just couldn't be overlooked—and that was murder.

The *valley* has never been so *sweet*!

Having left Sweet Valley High School behind them, Jessica and Elizabeth Wakefield have begun a new stage in their lives, attending the most popular university around – Sweet Valley University!

Join them and all their friends for fun, frolics and frights on *and* off campus.

Ask your bookseller for any titles you may have missed. The Sweet Valley University series is published by Bantam Books.

1. COLLEGE GIRLS
2. LOVE, LIES AND JESSICA WAKEFIELD
3. WHAT YOUR PARENTS DON'T KNOW
4. ANYTHING FOR LOVE
5. A MARRIED WOMAN
6. THE LOVE OF HER LIFE
7. GOOD-BYE TO LOVE
8. HOME FOR CHRISTMAS
9. SORORITY SCANDAL
10. NO MEANS NO
11. TAKE BACK THE NIGHT
12. COLLEGE CRUISE
13. SS HEARTBREAK
14. SHIPBOARD WEDDING
15. BEHIND CLOSED DOORS
16. THE OTHER WOMAN
17. DEADLY ATTRACTION
18. BILLIE'S SECRET
19. BROKEN PROMISES, SHATTERED DREAMS
20. HERE COMES THE BRIDE

THRILLER: WANTED FOR MURDER
THRILLER: HE'S WATCHING YOU
THRILLER: KISS OF THE VAMPIRE
THRILLER: THE HOUSE OF DEATH
THRILLER: RUNNING FOR HER LIFE

# SWEET VALLEY UNIVERSITY

## THRILLER EDITION

# *Running for Her Life*

### Written by
### Laurie John

### Created by
### FRANCINE PASCAL

BANTAM BOOKS
NEW YORK · TORONTO · LONDON · SYDNEY · AUCKLAND

# RUNNING FOR HER LIFE
## A BANTAM BOOK : 0 553 50451 7

Originally published in USA by Bantam Books

First publication in Great Britain

PRINTING HISTORY
Bantam edition published 1996

Conceived by Francine Pascal

Produced by Daniel Weiss Associates, Inc,
33 West 17th Street, New York, NY 10011

Bantam Books are published by Transworld Publishers Ltd,
61–63 Uxbridge Road, Ealing, London W5 5SA,
in Australia by Transworld Publishers (Australia) Pty Ltd,
15–25 Helles Avenue, Moorebank, NSW 2170,
and in New Zealand by Transworld Publishers (NZ) Ltd,
3 William Pickering Drive, Albany, Auckland.

Printed and bound in Great Britain by
Cox & Wyman Ltd, Reading, Berkshire.

*To Caitlin Walsh*

# Chapter One

"Move out of the way!" a woman shouted hysterically to a group of pedestrians crossing the street. "Here it comes!" she shrieked.

A second later a police car screamed around the corner, its rear tires burning against the pavement. It was clear that something was wrong. People scattered in haphazard directions.

"He's out of control!" a man yelled.

The police car lunged erratically, sideswiping a fruit stand. The vehicle seemed to be headed straight for a mother and child who were crossing the street, when at the last moment, a teenager frantically pulled them out of the way. Through the windshield, they could see the driver's terrified face as he spun the steering wheel wildly.

"It's coming this way!" someone screamed.

Elizabeth Wakefield and Tom Watts stared at the swerving car, their eyes wide and their bodies rigid, as it came closer. They froze in its path. Elizabeth gave Tom's hand a nervous squeeze, but didn't turn to look at him. She didn't dare break her gaze with the oncoming car.

Suddenly the police car veered sharply to the right, onto the highway overpass. Elizabeth held her breath as she watched it crash through the guardrail and sail through the air in a graceful arc. Seconds before it hit the highway below, a fuel truck appeared from under the bridge and the two vehicles collided in a fantastic explosion.

Elizabeth smiled excitedly at Tom as orange-yellow flames billowed across the screen. She reached over and grabbed a handful of buttery popcorn. Screeching guitars and a heavy drumbeat pounded from the movie theater speakers.

*"This summer, New Vision Studios will take you on a thrill ride you won't forget . . . ,"* the announcer's voice said over the throbbing music. On-screen, the figures of a man and a woman emerged from the fire, holding hands and running in slow motion. *". . . to a place where everyone is on the wrong side of the law, and no one can be trusted. . . ."* The woman's cascading curls flowed behind her as she ran, and hot fire licked the heels of her feet. *"Starring Julia Reynolds . . ."* The man's strong form was a dark shadow against the blaze. *". . . and Matt Barron . . . in* DEADLY IMPACT."

The movie's title was scrawled across the screen in bloodred letters before it exploded into a million pieces. Everything went black. *"Coming this summer to a theater near you."*

Elizabeth felt a gentle finger prodding her shoulder.

"Time to wake up, Liz," Tom said sweetly.

She groggily lifted her golden blond head off Tom's shoulder and blinked a few times until her eyes focused. The movie screen was white, and an army of ushers were picking up abandoned soda containers and sweeping up popcorn kernels. All of the seats were empty.

"The movie's over already?" Elizabeth said with a sleepy yawn.

Tom's brown eyes sparkled with amusement. "Already? It was almost two and a half hours."

She rubbed the sleep from her eyes. "How much did I miss?"

"Let's see"—Tom rubbed his chin thoughtfully—"I think you dozed off sometime between the sneak previews and the opening credits."

"That's pretty bad," Elizabeth groaned. She pulled out a lone Milk Dud that had worked its way into the pocket of her blue Sweet Valley University sweatshirt. "I'm sorry, Tom. I guess I'm not the most exciting person to spend an evening with."

Pulling her closer to him, Tom kissed Elizabeth softly on the lips. "I can't think of anyone I'd rather be with," he whispered as he looked deeply into her blue-green eyes. "Besides, you didn't miss

3

that much. It was a pretty boring movie. Even the previews seemed more interesting."

They walked hand in hand up the aisle. Elizabeth tossed the empty popcorn box into the trash can by the exit. "I did like the previews," she said brightly. "Especially the one for that new action movie. If that movie had been playing tonight, I know I wouldn't have fallen asleep."

Tom opened the door for Elizabeth. The cool, damp night air made her senses come alive. It had been dry outside before the movie, but now Elizabeth noticed that the pavement was slicked with fresh rain. Puddles dotted the parking lot, reflecting the orange glow of the floodlights.

"Don't forget to tell your sister about the movie," Tom said, carefully making his way through the maze of parked cars. "Especially since Julia Reynolds is in it. Jessica seems really interested in her lately."

Elizabeth ran her finger through a few beads of rainwater that had collected on the windshield of Tom's blue Saturn. "Interested isn't the word," she answered dryly. "With her, she's an obsession."

Jessica Wakefield unpinned the last of the hot rollers and watched it tumble onto the floor of the dorm room she shared with her twin sister, Elizabeth. With an admiring glance, she surveyed the single, spiraling, blond curl that dangled in front of her face.

"Not bad," she said, winking at her reflection. Jessica pouted thoughtfully at the glossy magazine cover propped up against her vanity mirror. In the latest issue of *Ingenue*, there was a photo of Julia Reynolds with her auburn hair piled glamorously on top of her head, a few stray curls cascading softly around her face. After four hours of practice, not only had Jessica been able to duplicate the style, she'd nearly perfected it.

"Now for the finishing touch." Jessica took a hairpin and, with the skilled precision of a brain surgeon, strategically pushed it into the mass of curls. She coated her hair with a generous dose of spray gel and smiled seductively at the mirror.

"Ms. Wakefield, how does it feel to be the toast of Hollywood?" a voice rang out.

Jessica whipped her head around, her hair staying firmly in place as she moved. She'd been so preoccupied with her hair that she hadn't even noticed that Elizabeth and Tom had returned from the movie.

"Do you like?" Jessica said, sucking in her cheeks.

Elizabeth's eyes dropped from her twin sister to the magazine photos of Julia Reynolds scattered on the floor. "You're a dead ringer," she said mechanically. "You could probably get a job as her stunt double."

Jessica beamed with satisfaction. "What do you think, Tom?"

Tom plopped down on the twins' small couch

and propped a pillow behind his head. "I think you'd better wear a disguise when you go out or you might be attacked by star-crazed photojournalists," he said with a smirk.

"I hope so," Jessica sighed contentedly. She treated herself to luxurious fantasies of fighting off the paparazzi and hearing international journalists begging for interviews. *Jessica Wakefield—the most sought-after woman in Hollywood.*

Taking a seat next to Tom, Elizabeth pulled out the flowered scrunchie in her hair and tossed it onto their makeshift coffee table. "We saw a preview tonight for a movie you'll have to see," she said, snuggling closer to Tom. "It stars Julia Reynolds."

The mention of Julia Reynolds's name snapped Jessica out of her musings. "Oh, you mean *Deadly Impact*?" She picked up her collection of gossip magazines and stacked them neatly on the corner of her cluttered desk. "Did it look good?"

"It looked great," Tom said. "Really cool. It's supposed to be out in midsummer."

"That is, if everything goes all right," Jessica answered with authority.

Elizabeth eyed her curiously. "What do you mean?"

Jessica stretched out on the floor, elbows bent and head resting in her hands. "Actually, the movie was supposed to be released this week, but the project's gone way over budget and there are still a few scenes that need to be reshot. If everything goes well, they'll finish editing by early summer, just in time for the summer action movie season."

Tom and Elizabeth exchanged knowing looks.

"The funny thing is," Jessica continued, unfazed. "Julia wasn't even supposed to do this movie. Originally, she had an exclusive contract with Mammoth Pictures for five years. But then, this new maverick movie company, New Vision Studios, offered her four million dollars to do *Deadly Impact*."

Tom let out a low whistle. "Whew, that's *a lot* of cash."

"I can't even imagine what I'd do with all that money," Elizabeth chimed in. "I'd probably give most of it to charity."

"I'm sure *I* could find a few *dozen* uses for it." Jessica's feet kicked wildly in the air. "So you can imagine how easy the decision was for Julia. She broke her contract with Mammoth and signed on with New Vision."

"Is there anything else about Julia Reynolds we should know?" Elizabeth asked, trying to stifle a yawn.

Jessica's eyes lifted dreamily to the ceiling. "She's engaged to her longtime boyfriend, Matt Barron, the other star of *Deadly Impact*. It's rumored that they're going to get hitched in the next few weeks."

The corner of Tom's mouth turned up in a smirk. "I've got to hand it to you, Jess. You've certainly done your homework."

Jessica twirled a fat curl around her finger. "I have to learn everything I can about this business," she said in a serious tone. "After all, I'm going to be the next Julia Reynolds."

Ronald Bishop paced the deep-piled carpet of his sprawling forty-second-floor office. Beads of sweat trickled from his graying temples to the creases in his plump neck.

"It's stuffy in here," he mumbled to himself, patting his brow with the red silk handkerchief he always kept tucked in the breast pocket of his imported Italian suit. According to the thermostat, the office was at the same temperature it had been for twenty years, but today, Ronald turned the air conditioner up another notch.

There was a light knock at the door. Bishop ignored it as he opened the wooden cigar box on the corner of his highly polished desk and shoved an unlit cigar into the corner of his mouth.

The door creaked open. "You wanted to see me, sir?"

Bishop cleared his throat loudly. "I see you got my memo, Pierce," he said, his voice filling every corner of the office. He sucked pensively on the cigar as he watched the well-dressed young man standing awkwardly by the door. "Don't just stand there—have a seat."

Rodney Pierce's dark mustache twitched nervously. He unbuttoned the jacket of his pinstriped suit and sat in the middle of the burgundy . leather couch. "Yeah, McKenna briefed me on the rest."

"Good, good." Bishop nodded almost imperceptibly. He leaned his heavy torso against the desk for support. "So what do you think?"

Pierce rested his right ankle on his left knee and ran a hand through his slick black hair. "I don't know," he said timorously.

"What do you mean, you don't know?" Bishop's unkempt eyebrows knitted in agitation. "Are you up for it or not?"

"Why even bother asking me that question?" Pierce shifted in his seat. "It's not like I have a choice in the matter."

Bishop's teeth sank into the tip of the cigar. "Of course you have a choice," he said ominously. "You can choose to go along with the plans I've laid out for you, or you can choose to spend the rest of your life wasting away in prison." He opened the top drawer of his desk and pulled out a large yellow envelope. "Don't forget—if I go down, you're going with me." He let the words hang in the air like a storm cloud.

Pierce swallowed hard. He stared at the envelope for a long time. "What's my first assignment?" he asked finally.

A twisted smile broke across Bishop's face. He handed the envelope to the anxious young man. "You know how much is at stake, Pierce. Don't disappoint me."

With shaking fingers, Pierce broke the seal on

the envelope. His eyes bulged as he scanned the information inside.

Bishop laughed. "By this time tomorrow, New Vision will be sinking fast."

"I can't believe it's only a week away!" Julia Reynolds said excitedly. Her sensuous lips parted in a broad smile as she watched her fiancé enter the dressing room.

"Hi, sweetheart," Matt Barron said. Carefully, he stepped behind Julia and kissed her on the back of the neck.

Martin, the makeup artist who'd been working on Julia's face for nearly an hour, sighed in exasperation as he wiped away a smudge of lipstick that was on Julia's teeth. "You have to stay still, sweetie," Martin scolded gently. "I'll be done in just a minute—as long as you don't move."

"Sorry," Julia said without moving her lips. She reached for Matt's hand and gave it a squeeze.

Martin blotted Julia's lips. "All done, but don't be smooching with your honey unless you want me to spend another two hours on you." Martin gave her a wink, then moved on to the next actor.

Finally free, Julia turned to Matt. "Can you believe it? In a week, we're going to be married!"

Matt's golden eyes sparkled. He brought Julia's hand to his mouth and softly kissed her fingertips. "You're not getting cold feet on me, are you?"

"Never," she said, looking away coyly. A lock of auburn hair fell against her porcelain complexion, and at that very moment, Matt was certain she was the most beautiful woman on earth. "I just meant that a week isn't a lot of time to finish everything we need to do for the ceremony."

Matt pushed his brown chin-length hair away from his face. It fell in a natural part down the middle of his scalp, perfectly framing his chiseled features. "We booked the church and the reception hall. You have a dress and I have a new tux— what's left to worry about?"

Julia's .striking green eyes flashed him a look that instantly made his heart melt. "You have absolutely no idea what it takes to put on a wedding," she said with a hint of accusation.

Helen, Julia's hairdresser, stood behind Julia and ran her fingers through the star's thick curls. She sprayed different sections of Julia's hair with a squirt bottle and coaxed it into smooth ringlets.

Julia's head moved easily from side to side as the short hairdresser worked around her. "There are hundreds of details that need to be taken care of," she said to Matt.

Matt scratched the dark stubble on his chin, looking a bit perplexed. "What kind of details?"

Julia crossed her long, curvaceous legs. "Flowers for one—I still haven't had a chance to pick out the flower arrangements for the ceremony. Can you imagine a wedding without flowers?"

"Who'll even notice the flowers with the most gorgeous woman in the world standing at the altar?" he said sincerely.

Julia bit her lip. "If I didn't have all this makeup on my face, I'd kiss you right now."

"Stop it, you two," Helen snapped. "I can't take it anymore! You're making me and everyone else in this place jealous."

"She's not kidding," Meghan, Julia's personal assistant, said as she walked into the room carrying a clipboard and a bottle of seltzer water. Meghan handed Julia the bottle of seltzer. "They need you in five minutes."

Julia unscrewed the cap and carefully drank the water through a straw without letting a drop of it touch her lips. "Where am I supposed to be?"

Fanning herself with a rainbow-colored New Vision Studios baseball cap, Meghan pointed out the area on the studio-lot map. "It's on lot number two, where all the building facades are," she said, her finger tracing the path. "It's the same facade they used yesterday. Go around the back and climb the ladder to the fourth level, then wait for directions. Someone's supposed to meet you there to guide you through the jump."

Julia laughed aloud and took another drink of seltzer. Matt instantly detected a note of nervousness in her voice.

"You don't have to do it," he said, as if reading her thoughts. "Just say the word, and they'll put in your stunt double, instead."

"No, no—I like the challenge," Julia said casually. She turned to Meghan. "Tell them I'll be there right away. And thanks for the seltzer."

Meghan tucked the clipboard under her arm and marched back out to the studio lot.

"Are you sure you want to do the jump?" Matt said. His catlike eyes darkened with concern.

"It's fine, really," she said with a dismissive wave. As she moved her hand, the enormous diamond engagement ring Matt had given her glimmered under the fluorescent lights of the trailer. "Besides, I want to get over my fear of heights so we can go skiing in the French alps on our honeymoon."

Matt's heart was so full, he thought it might burst. The next week was going to seem like an eternity. "Be careful out there on the platform," he said, kissing Julia tenderly on the forehead. "I'll be waiting for you on the other side."

"Places, everybody!" the director shouted into the air.

Matt took a seat in a folding chair behind camera one. Directly in front of him, the enormous building facade rose four full stories. It was a replica of the old brownstone apartment buildings he'd seen in Manhattan on his last movie shoot. The facade looked amazingly real, even though it was only a steel frame covered with painted plaster and Styrofoam.

"Julia? Are you almost ready?" The director spoke through a megaphone so that his voice would carry to the fourth-floor window where Julia was standing.

Julia peered out of the window frame. She leaned over timidly, looking down at the huge air mattress waiting to break her fall. Even from a distance, Matt could tell that she was anxious. "Are you okay?" he shouted up to her.

Julia nodded weakly.

Matt walked over to the side of the mattress. "I'll be right here!" he called, hoping to make her feel a little better.

"Are you sure you want to go through with this?" the director asked, straightening the visor of his baseball cap.

Julia gave him a thumbs-up sign.

"What I need you to do is to keep out of sight—stay away from the window," the director explained. "Is someone there to give you the signal?"

Julia turned around, then gave another thumbs-up sign.

The director took a seat behind the camera. "As soon as he gives you the signal, take the jump. The best way for you to do it is to get a running start," he called. "Are you ready?"

Julia waved to both of them, then stepped away from the window, out of sight. Matt's strong jaw tensed. He couldn't wait for this scene to be over.

"Quiet on the set!" the director bellowed. "Cameras rolling . . . and action!"

*"Wait!"* Matt yelled. The word escaped him almost immediately, and yet he was afraid it wasn't

soon enough. For a few sickening seconds, he'd waited to see Julia appear in the window and tumble to the earth, only to look down and find that there was a rip in the air mattress. It couldn't have supported her.

"Hold it, everybody!" the director shouted into the megaphone. He walked over to where Matt was standing. "What is it, big guy? Wedding jitters?"

Matt's eyes darted around the set. *Julia's fine,* he repeated over and over again to himself. *She didn't take the jump.* "It's the mattress," he said, pointing a shaky finger at it. "There's a huge tear in the side."

"Well I'll be—" In an instant, the veins in the director's neck were popping out, and he was shouting at every person who crossed his path. "Why didn't someone make sure the mattress was safe to use? Don't you people realize that you put someone's life in danger because of your carelessness?"

Matt gripped his throbbing head with his hands. *What would've happened if I hadn't seen the tear?* His mind reeled at the horrific thought. A cold chill seized his body. The only thing that mattered to him was to be married to Julia, to share his life with her. The thought that it had almost been cruelly snatched away from him left Matt with a sour ache in the pit of his stomach.

Julia's figure emerged from behind the window. She waved sullenly at Matt from above. He knew that the mishap must have deeply disturbed her.

"Don't do it." Matt mouthed the words, hoping she'd get the message.

Julia's face wrinkled in confusion. "What?" she mouthed back.

"Don't . . . jump." Matt spoke slowly and deliberately, concentrating all his energy into sending the message to her. He didn't care about skiing in the French alps—he just wanted Julia safe and in one piece.

Four crew members dragged off the defective air mattress. "Give me a minute and we'll have a brand-new one set up, Julia," the director said evenly into the megaphone.

Julia waved down at Matt. He tried one more time to send her the message. She must not have understood, because she just shrugged her shoulders and blew him a big kiss. Then she disappeared behind the window again.

The air was unseasonably warm and humid for early spring, and it pressed down on Matt like an oppressive weight. His lungs struggled to take in the heavy air. The heat from the pavement burned through the soles of his leather cowboy boots. The four crew members had dropped completely out of sight, in search of a new air mattress. Everyone on the set was quiet.

Then, in an earth-shattering second, it happened.

Matt looked up to see Julia run and leap out

the window with all her strength. She looked straight out over the lot, her face filled with excitement and bold determination at successfully executing the jump. In the next instant, he saw Julia look down at the rushing pavement. Matt watched in horror as the realization swept over her face.

*"Noooo!"* Julia's mouth opened, and a terrifying scream tore from her throat as she fell. Suddenly, the ghastly sound stopped.

"Someone, call an ambulance!" the director barked.

Dark red blood trickled into the cracks in the pavement, flowing like hundreds of tiny, gruesome rivers. Matt raced to Julia's side, his numb fingers searching for the slightest flicker of a heartbeat. But even before he touched her, Matt knew the frightening truth: Julia was dead.

# Chapter Two

"Last night was a complete disaster," Nina Harper declared during breakfast as she pulled the top off a container of strawberry yogurt.

Elizabeth stared at her best friend with intrigue. "What happened?" she asked, spearing a sausage link from Tom's plate.

Nina's beaded braids clicked as she tossed them over her shoulder. "I was all set to do major studying in the library," she said as she stirred the yogurt. "I had the research materials I needed, a brand-new pack of pens, and a smuggled cup of coffee. Then Bryan came over, and we chatted for a while."

Elizabeth smiled slyly. "Sounds good so far."

The corners of Nina's mouth turned down. "Then some of his friends stopped by my table, and next thing I know, we're drawing a crowd. Two hours must've gone by before everyone left."

"Did you get any work done after?" Tom said, taking a sip of grapefruit juice.

"No, it gets worse," Nina said. Her brow furrowed. "As soon as I was alone again, I opened my art history text. And that's the last thing I remember. The security guard woke me up at one in the morning, when they were closing. My head was resting on the same page I had started on." She ate a spoonful of yogurt. "The real kicker is, the guard saw the illegal coffee on my table and gave me a fine."

"Ouch! What a bad break," Elizabeth answered. The students at the other end of the cafeteria table collected their things and left. Elizabeth reached over and grabbed the newspaper they'd left. "But your body's telling you you're working too hard again, Nina. You should've gone to the movies with us last night."

"You're probably right," Nina nodded. "I spent the whole night in the library, and all I have to show for it is a stiff neck and a fifteen-dollar fine."

Elizabeth pulled off the front section of the newspaper. At the exact same moment, Nina and Tom lunged for the comics, tugging at opposite corners of the paper.

"Hey, Nina, I'll give you a bite of my French toast if you let me look at it first," Tom coaxed, eagerly eyeing the colorful pages.

"No dice." Nina gave the comics a quick tug in her direction. "Cold, hard cash or nothing."

19

Tom smiled mischievously. "Did I tell you how much I like your new bracelet?"

Nina stifled a laugh as her eyes dropped to the plain silver bangle on her wrist. "I've worn this bracelet almost every day since the beginning of school." She squinted and focused on something just over Tom's shoulder. "You won't believe who just walked through the cafeteria door . . ."

"Oh, wow!" Elizabeth exclaimed.

Just as Tom whipped around to see who it was, Nina yanked the comics out of his hand. "Who?" he asked, hardly realizing he'd lost it. His eyes darted around the room.

A self-satisfied smirk crossed Nina's lips. "He's gone now."

Tom stared ruefully. "Don't tell me . . ."

"Yep, you've been had." Nina folded the paper in half. "With many thanks to my good friend Elizabeth."

"Thanks, Liz," Tom said.

Elizabeth's eyes were fixed on the front page. "I wasn't intentionally trying to help her, I was looking at the headline." She held up the paper so they both could see: MOVIE ACTRESS COMMITS SUICIDE ON SET.

Nina dropped the comics. Tom's fingers slid stealthily across the tabletop and snagged the paper without her noticing. "Who was it?" Nina asked.

"Julia Reynolds."

"No way!" Tom's eyes bulged. "What happened?"

Elizabeth scanned the article for details. "They're not sure. Apparently, she was supposed to do a stunt, and she jumped before the safety mattress was put in place."

"How weird!" Nina reached for the comics in front of her, only to find they were missing. "Can you imagine killing yourself in front of all those people?"

Elizabeth puckered her lips thoughtfully. "It says here that she didn't even leave a suicide note."

"I don't get the whole Hollywood mentality," Tom interjected. Creases formed over his eyebrows. "How can people who are rich and famous be so unhappy?"

"It's simple," Nina answered. "When you have everything, there's nothing else to look forward to. People in those situations often end up doing extreme things."

Jessica sauntered up behind Nina and plopped her orange cafeteria tray on the table. A catlike pair of tortoiseshell sunglasses covered her eyes. "Who did something extreme?" she asked, worming her way into the conversation. "I just love a juicy bit of gossip first thing in the morning."

A look of alarm passed between Nina and Elizabeth while Tom hid his face behind the comics.

Jessica nibbled daintily at a croissant. "Don't keep me waiting, guys. Spill it."

Elizabeth reached over and removed her sister's sunglasses. They looked exactly like the ones Julia Reynolds was wearing in the newspaper photo. "Jess, I've got some bad news," she said delicately. "It's about Julia."

Jessica stopped chewing. Her blue-green eyes flitted from side to side, as if she were trying to glean some information from their faces. "What? Did she call off the wedding?"

Elizabeth bit the inside of her cheek. Jessica's obsession with the movie star seemed so childish, but Elizabeth's heart went out to her just the same. "Julia Reynolds committed suicide yesterday."

Jessica's smile froze, and for several seconds, Elizabeth thought that maybe she hadn't heard right. Then suddenly, her expression changed; her mouth took on a hard line, and her eyes had an icy edge. "Very funny," she said snidely.

Nina pointed to the front page of the newspaper. "She's not making it up, Jess."

A slight wrenching feeling churned in Elizabeth's stomach as she watched her twin's eyes fill with tears. It was the same sensation she'd felt when they were kids and Jessica had skinned her knee or been grounded for disobeying their parents. No matter what the reason was, it pained Elizabeth to see her sister upset.

"I'm really sorry, Jess," Elizabeth said as she watched her absorb the details of the article.

"Poor Matt," Jessica whispered, her voice thick with emotion. "He must be devastated." She wiped away a tear that traced a path down her cheek. "How could she do this when her wedding was only a week away?"

"I don't know," Elizabeth answered, gazing at the photo. The glowing, confident smile of the movie star stared back at them, unable to reveal any clues to the mystery. There could've been any number of reasons why she'd wanted to end her life—but why now, when everything seemed so perfect?

Elizabeth shook her head and looked away. "I guess we'll never know."

"Well done!" Richard McKenna boomed as he barged into Pierce's tiny office. Proudly, he held up the morning newspaper like a banner. "You did a good, clean job. No one will suspect a thing."

Pierce's eyes rested on the word *suicide* that was printed over Julia's photo. A slow, burning fluid trickled down his throat. Pierce bared his teeth at McKenna in disgust. "What do *you* want?"

McKenna ran a pale hand through his thinning red hair and took a seat in the straight chair next to Pierce's metal desk. "I heard your scheme was nearly spoiled when good old Matt Barron discovered the tear in the air mattress." McKenna laced his fingers and rested his hands against the expanse of his broad belly. "But I'm glad to see you didn't let that little hitch stop you. Great comeback!"

Impulsively, Pierce smoothed down his mustache and peered through the cracked door that connected his office to Ronald Bishop's.

"Don't worry," McKenna said coolly. "Your

boss isn't back from lunch yet. You know you can always talk freely with me."

Pierce breathed in the stale office air, hoping to clear the fuzziness that was clouding his head. His palms were continually moist, no matter how many times he brushed them against the pockets of his suit jacket. Everything Pierce saw took on a strange, nightmarish quality, as though he were looking at the world through a fun-house mirror. "Please, just get to the point," he said impatiently. "I'm not feeling too well right now."

McKenna nodded condescendingly. "It's just nerves. You'll be fine by tomorrow." His doughy face broke into a wide grin. "As executive vice president of Mammoth Pictures, I wanted to thank you for your fine effort in helping the company maintain its position at the top of the industry," he said in a formal tone as he extended his hand toward Pierce. "I just hope Bishop realizes what a dutiful assistant he has. Good old Gilbert Bradley's been working for me for six years, and I can't even get him to bring me a cup of coffee!"

Pierce glared at McKenna's ghostly hand, feeling like the winner in some bizarre game show. "I wish that were all my boss asked me to do," he said quietly.

"No, I think Bishop's right in involving you so much in his affairs." McKenna retracted his unshaken hand without batting an eye. "It shows that he has a great deal of faith in you."

The corners of Pierce's mouth turned down as

he focused on the blank white wall above McKenna's head. "When I first came here, I thought my job would be to assist Mr. Bishop in the running of this company. I had no idea that I'd be involved with his gambling activities or that I'd have to help him cover his tracks with the company money he used."

"But Bishop and his circle of friends are very grateful to you," McKenna said. "Myself included."

"I don't care who's grateful—it's wrong!" Pierce snapped.

McKenna's belly bobbed up and down as he laughed. "It's a little late for you to suddenly develop a conscience."

Pierce's stomach heaved as he remembered the day before, out on the movie lot. He had been standing on the fourth level behind the building facade, pretending to be receiving instructions from the director through his headpiece. Julia waited nervously for the jump, her hair catching the light of the scorching California sun. *"Don't worry,"* he had told her. *"I'll let you know when it's safe to jump."* Seconds later he was giving her a false signal, and Julia took a running jump out of the window. Even standing on the fourth level, he could hear her sickening scream and the grisly thud of her body slamming against the pavement.

"I'm not the one who decided Julia needed to die," Pierce said a moment later, trying to push the memory out of his head.

"But you're the one who killed her."

"It's not like I had much of a choice," Pierce retorted.

McKenna's dull green eyes surveyed him harshly. "You always have a choice," he said bluntly. "And you chose to be loyal to your boss and to protect his reputation." McKenna stood up and smoothed the wrinkles from his suit. "If we can keep a lid on the investigation, you'll be able to resume a normal life and put this whole thing behind you." A shadow crossed his face. "But I want to warn you that if word should get out, you'd better be prepared for your next assignment. We can't afford to have any speculation from the public."

Hot blood rushed to Pierce's brain. "There won't be a 'next assignment.' I refuse to do it again."

McKenna rested his white fists on the desktop and leaned forward on his soft knuckles. Pierce could feel McKenna's breath on his face. "You will finish what you started," he commanded.

"You just finished saying that I always have a choice." The words caught in Pierce's throat. "I *choose* not to do it again."

"It's much too late to back out now. Bishop can't risk having you squeal. Either you do as you're told, or he'll see that you're thrown in prison," McKenna barked. "Bishop's got some pretty powerful friends."

Sweat collected in the creases of Pierce's palms,

loosening his grip on the desk's edge. "Bishop threatened me with prison before," he scoffed with false bravado. "I'm not going to fall for it this time."

A blue vein pulsed at McKenna's temple. "If I were you, I wouldn't be so cavalier about the situation," he said. "Before, when you were loosely tied to Bishop's gambling, there was very little evidence to convict you of anything. There was no way it would even hold up in court." McKenna leaned over, his puffy face only inches away from Pierce. "But now they can get you for murder."

"I'm home!" Elizabeth said in a light voice as she hung up her jean jacket on the coatrack near the door. All the lights were off, except for a single lamp illuminating her sister's desktop.

Jessica was slumped over a stack of magazines—all of which bore boldly printed headlines of Julia Reynolds's suicide. "Hey," Jessica said without looking up from her desk. "What's up?"

Elizabeth clicked on the switch for the overhead light. "I brought you a present," she said, carrying over a white cardboard box. She placed the box on the only clear spot on Jessica's desk. "Since you wouldn't go out with me for dessert, I figured I'd bring it to you."

Jessica rubbed her red-rimmed eyes. "What is it?" she asked groggily.

Elizabeth nudged the box closer to her. "Open it and find out."

Pushing a magazine aside, Jessica lifted the lid. Her face lit up at the sight of the rich, chocolaty dessert. "Mississippi mud cake," she said with a smile. "Thanks, this is great."

Elizabeth loosened her ponytail and kicked off her penny loafers. Her gaze traveled from Jessica's dessert to a full-color photo of Julia Reynolds with the words DEATH OF A RISING STAR printed in bold, red letters. Elizabeth picked up the magazine and flipped through it. "Looks like you've been pretty busy while I've been out."

Jessica ate a forkful of cake. "I'm just trying to find one good reason why Julia would do something like that, especially since everything was going so well for her."

"I doubt you'll get any real answers from a magazine." Elizabeth glanced through the montage of photos taken a week before the star's death with morbid fascination. The playful, glamorous shots that were supposed to be used to promote her new movie suddenly took on a dark significance. "It's hard to know what to believe."

"They all basically say the same thing—that she committed suicide, but that no one knows why," Jessica said. She licked a bit of chocolate from her fingers. "The gossip papers are reporting that Julia had a history of depression, and that's why she did it."

"It all sounds like speculation to me." Elizabeth sat down on the couch, hugging a round, floral-print pillow. "Cynthia Zartman, my

28

journalism professor, says that those sleazy magazines thrive on half-truths and false assumptions. You can't believe a word of it."

"I don't," Jessica said, staring intensely at her sister. "In fact, I have my own theory."

Elizabeth's eyes narrowed. "And what's that?"

"I think it was all a big accident. Julia jumped at the wrong time, it's as simple as that." She waved her fork in the air to illustrate the point. "But everyone's overlooked that idea."

Elizabeth bolted upright. Jessica could be on to something. "Or maybe the movie studio is keeping the whole thing under wraps," she said. "Think about it—if you just signed on a huge movie star and she died because of some stupid mistake, the whole company could go down."

One of Jessica's eyebrows arched thoughtfully. "Yeah, maybe you're right. New Vision could lose millions over this," she agreed. "The accident theory is a strong possibility."

*But it's not the only one,* Elizabeth thought to herself. Clearly, the idea of suicide just didn't seem to fit. Jessica was right, it *could've* been an accident. But a growing uneasiness in Elizabeth's gut told her that the whole situation could go much deeper than anyone was willing to admit. In the high-stakes world of Hollywood, there was one possibility that just couldn't be overlooked—and that was murder.

"I have Governor Dawson on line three," Pierce said, poking his head into Bishop's office.

The color seemed to have drained from his face. "Will you take it?"

Bishop's meaty jaw tensed. "Put him on," he said flatly. "And close the door behind you."

Pierce nodded. He backed out of the room with a faltering step and closed the door. As soon as the red light flashed on Bishop's telephone, he grabbed the receiver.

"Hey there, George." Bishop forced a lilt in his voice to cover up the foul mood he was in. "I didn't expect to hear from you. Don't tell me it's election time already."

The governor laughed with the smooth precision of a politician. "I never stop fund-raising. You know that."

Bishop leaned back in his swivel chair, crossing his thick legs at the ankles. "I thought you did all your fund-raising at the racetrack."

"To tell you the truth, I do miss playing the horses," the governor said wistfully. "But I decided it wouldn't be too healthy for my political future if I kept it up."

"Well, if you ever decide to go back to it, you know where we are," Bishop answered. "The boys and I miss seeing you down at the track. McKenna's always asking me when you're coming back."

"Tell him not to worry about me. He should be worrying about Mammoth Pictures, instead," the governor replied. "And that's why I'm calling you. I heard the news about Julia Reynolds. What a terrible tragedy."

Bishop's upper lip curled in a sneer. Not only was the governor good at trying to sound friendly, he could fake sympathy, as well. "It certainly is a sad situation," Bishop said with caution. "Senseless, too. Obviously, New Vision has a lot to learn about handling big-name talent." Sweat dampened Bishop's forehead. His voice dropped to a confidential tone. "Between you and me, I have a feeling Julia got in way over her head with that bunch of amateurs. Once she realized she was on a one-way track to wrecking her career, she had to bail out."

The governor cleared his throat. "So you're saying this wouldn't have happened if she'd stayed with your studio?"

Bishop's face burned with anger. He felt as though he were suddenly being cross-examined by a shrewd lawyer. "What I'm saying is that by breaking her contract with us, Julia made the biggest mistake of her life," he snapped. "Mammoth Pictures is a class act. We know how to deal with big stars. New Vision doesn't have a prayer."

"Maybe so," the governor answered. "But some of your biggest stars are crossing over to New Vision. If I were you, I'd be a bit more concerned."

Bishop pulled out his red silk handkerchief and dabbed his forehead. "As soon as they find out they're getting a raw deal, they'll come crawling back."

"Just promise me I won't be reading about them in the papers."

A spastic laugh escaped Bishop's lips. "I'm not exactly sure what you're getting at, Governor, but let me assure you that Julia's death was no surprise to any of us here. Julia Reynolds was a troubled young woman." Impulsively, he reached for the wooden cigar box. "If I were you, I wouldn't waste any tax dollars on such a cut-and-dried case. I'm sure your investigators would prefer some real work."

There was a chill in the governor's voice. "I can't condone your business practices."

"I'm not asking you to agree with me," Bishop countered. "I'm only asking you to look the other way."

"Watch yourself," the governor answered. "Before you know it, you'll be in too deep."

Bishop leaned back in his chair and lit the cigar. "Thank you for your concern, Governor," he said, blowing a blue puff of smoke high into the air. "And be sure to call back when election time rolls around. You know who to count on in '98."

# Chapter Three

"Don't take everything at face value; learn to be critical readers." Professor Cynthia Zartman moved away from the chalkboard and leaned against the back of a chair. Her shiny black hair was pulled back into a loose braid that fell to the middle of her back. "Everyone has a political agenda these days, including the media."

Elizabeth scribbled furiously in her journalism notebook. While she enjoyed every one of her classes, Elizabeth looked forward to Professor Zartman's class the most. Not only was Zartman a fascinating lecturer, but the class dealt with issues that would affect Elizabeth's future career. Her dream was to become an investigative reporter.

Professor Zartman put her hands into the pockets of her maroon blazer and paced the floor at the front of the classroom. "Even statistics can be manipulated to fit any purpose or idea that a journalist wants to get across," she said. "Therefore, when you're reading an article, it's important to identify the journalist's slant and then to think about the other viewpoint that's not being expressed."

Elizabeth stopped writing for a moment and stared blankly at the wall. Professor Zartman's comments sent Elizabeth's mind reeling back to the night before, when she and Jessica had been talking about Julia Reynolds's death. After reading dozens of articles, Jessica had said that nearly all the magazines and newspapers were reporting the same story.

*"They all basically say the same thing,"* she'd said. *"That Julia committed suicide, but that no one knows why."*

Even though Elizabeth was troubled by the evidence, and Jessica didn't believe it was a suicide, no one was writing anything to the contrary. If every newspaper in the country maintained that Julia's death was a suicide, did that make it an absolute truth?

Zartman erased the notes she had written on the chalkboard. "To illustrate my point, I'm giving you an assignment for our next class," the professor announced.

A few low groans echoed from the back of the room.

Professor Zartman smirked. "Don't get all worked up. I think you'll find this assignment interesting," she said. "The amount of time you put into it is entirely up to you; all I ask is that you are thorough and you document your sources."

Elizabeth flipped her notebook to a clean page, her pen poised in midair. A mild thrill of anticipation ran through her. Whenever she worked on a journalism assignment, Elizabeth usually became completely absorbed by it. She couldn't wait for the day when she would become a full-fledged journalist.

"I want you to find a current story in the papers and identify the slant," Professor Zartman continued. "Then I want you to write your *own* article on the same subject, expressing a different viewpoint. Your job is to find the story that isn't being reported." The professor turned and wrote a few words on the chalkboard. "It doesn't matter what you write about, as long as your article is well researched and your facts are checked." Zartman closed her briefcase, which always signaled the end of class. Without a moment's hesitation, a few students raced out the door. "Have fun with it," she finished.

A freshman hunk with sandy blond hair turned to the girl who was sitting directly in front of Elizabeth. "I have no idea what I'm going to write about. Do you?"

The girl shook her head as she shoved her notebook into her green backpack. "I'll probably pick something easy. I saw an article in the paper this morning about composting and organic gardening in northern California. Maybe I'll do that."

The blond guy laughed. "It's not too controversial,

but I bet you can get it done in two hours."

"That's the point," the girl said, getting up to leave.

Elizabeth made a few last-minute notes in her notebook and smiled to herself. She already knew what her paper topic was going to be—and it wasn't farming. Elizabeth was determined to find the real story behind Julia Reynolds's death.

"I'll always love you," Matt Barron murmured under his breath as he placed the single red rose on Julia's glossy wooden casket. One of the rose's thorns sank deeply into the flesh of his thumb, but Matt didn't flinch. The sharp, throbbing pain in his finger was no match for the searing pain in his heart.

Bridget Conners, Matt's publicist, touched him lightly on the elbow. "Are you all right?" she whispered to him as the minister recited the final prayer.

Matt shook his head silently as he watched Julia's body being lowered into the earth. Hot tears rolled down his face. *Good-bye, Julia,* he thought painfully. *Maybe we'll be together again some day.*

The minister closed his Bible, and the crowd slowly began to disperse.

"Here, take this." Bridget handed Matt a handkerchief. "Can I get you anything? Is there anything you need?"

Matt struggled to get the words out. His

throat felt as if it were collapsing upon itself. "No, but thanks." He wiped his face. At the moment he lifted his head to look around, a burst of white light exploded in his eyes.

"Mr. Barron, how are you feeling right now?" a reporter asked, shoving a microphone in his face.

Matt rubbed his eyes as they recovered from the blinding flashes of camera bulbs. Bridget gripped Matt's elbow and started to lead him through the labyrinth of reporters. *Go away,* he thought tiredly. *Just go away.*

"Mr. Barron has no comment at this time," Bridget answered firmly as she pushed on through the crowd.

Matt opened his eyes. They were still blurred from tears and flashes of light. Through the haze, he saw a flurry of hands thrusting microphones in front of him. He heard the furious clicking of camera shutters. Everyone seemed to be talking at once.

"What did you do to Julia to make her want to kill herself?" another reporter asked.

Someone to Matt's right grabbed at his shoulder. "Don't you feel responsible for her death?"

Matt balled his hands into tight, seething fists. He wanted to lash out, to smash their cameras and recorders, to break everything in his path. He wanted them to feel the same pain he was feeling at that very moment. *Then we'll see how many questions they ask,* he thought angrily.

But he didn't lash out. Instead, Matt walked

stiffly toward his waiting limo, following behind Bridget's black sun hat. His arms dangled limply at his sides. Despite the rage that was building inside him, Matt didn't have the energy to take action. Julia's death had drained him completely.

Another lightbulb flashed. "Are you seeing anyone new?" a voice called out.

"Leave Mr. Barron alone!" Bridget shouted harshly. "He has no comments at this time!" She opened the limo door, and they both slipped inside.

Bridget locked the door. "I can't believe this," she said, taking off her hat and placing it on her lap. "They're absolute animals."

Matt stared glassily through the tinted windows. Reporters continued to press themselves against the limo. Matt looked in fascination, slightly comforted by that fact that he could see out, but they couldn't see in.

"Where to?" the limo driver called.

Bridget poured Matt a glass of water from the bar. "Where do you want to go?" she asked him.

Matt watched the ice cubes in his water glass swirl around and around in endless circles. "It doesn't matter," he said.

"Now I know what a recycling bin feels like," Elizabeth said to herself with a hysterical laugh. She looked around at the mountain of papers and magazines surrounding her. It all added up to a small fortune, but that was the price you had to pay for thorough research.

"TRAGEDY AT NEW VISION STUDIOS," Elizabeth read from the cover of *CinemaScope*, the industry's leading trade magazine. She flipped to the article on page thirty-one, and Elizabeth's trained eye scanned the story.

"Here's a new one, Claude," Elizabeth said to the stuffed penguin that sat on her bookshelf. Claude wore a red satin bow tie decorated with white hearts and a matching cummerbund. The penguin had been a birthday present from Tom. "Ronald Bishop—he's the CEO of Mammoth Pictures. I suppose he's another person I should find out about." Elizabeth rubbed her itchy eyes and added Ronald Bishop's name to her list of people to be cross-referenced. Then she unfolded a huge chart and spread it over the piles of clippings and papers. Elizabeth had spent all night putting together the diagram showing the relationships of various people in the industry who were associated either directly or indirectly with Julia Reynolds.

"He must go right over here—" Elizabeth followed the left side of the chart, representing the chain of command at Mammoth Pictures. Elizabeth drew an arrow going up from Richard McKenna, the executive vice president, and connected it to Ronald Bishop's name at the very top. Elizabeth showed her work to the penguin. "So, Claude, what do you think?"

"Who are you talking to in there?" Tom's voice called from the other side of the door.

Elizabeth smiled. "It's my other boyfriend," she said coyly. "I'm hiding him from you."

"So that's why you won't let me in," Tom sighed. "What's his name?"

Elizabeth tore out the magazine article and added it to her pile of clippings. "Claude."

"Claude?" Tom said incredulously. "You'd leave me for a guy named *Claude*?"

"He's very well dressed," Elizabeth said with a laugh. She cracked open her fifth cola and poured it into a mug.

"Hey, Liz, it's Nina!" Nina's voice came through clearer than Tom's, because Nina liked to talk through the crack in the door. Elizabeth heard Nina trying to turn the doorknob, but it was locked. "When are you going to let us in?"

Elizabeth glanced proudly at the enormous chart spread out over her desk. In the last twenty-seven hours, she had made a great deal of progress. "As soon as I'm done!" Elizabeth called.

"Have you gotten any sleep since the last time we stopped by?" Nina asked.

Elizabeth opened another magazine. "Not a wink."

"You can't do this to yourself," Tom said with concern. Elizabeth could tell that he, too, had decided to start speaking through the crack in the door. "You need to get some sleep."

"I need to get this done," Elizabeth said,

tearing out another article. "I was pretty tired around five this morning, but over the last few hours, I've gotten my second wind." Elizabeth let out a cackling laugh. "I thinking I'm running on adrenaline."

"Caffeine and sugar is more like it," Nina said in a disapproving tone. "Girl, when you crash, you're going to crash *hard*."

"I don't care," Elizabeth said, taking another gulp of soda. "As long as my project is done, it doesn't matter." She scribbled a few names down on her notepad. "Did I tell you how fascinating this whole thing is?"

"When was the last time you ate something?" Tom asked. "You must be starved."

Elizabeth dropped her pen. She hadn't thought about food in hours, but the second he mentioned it, her stomach responded with a growl. "A little," she said.

"We brought your favorite sandwich from the deli," Tom said triumphantly.

Elizabeth's mouth started to water. "Dill chicken with tomatoes on a pita?"

"And we got you a surprise dessert," Nina added mysteriously.

"What is it?" Elizabeth asked, staring at the door.

"You'll just have to come out and see," Nina coaxed.

Elizabeth felt herself being drawn to the door. She stood there, her cheek pressed against the smooth wood. "Thanks for doing this for me, you guys. I really appreciate it." As she reached over to unlock the door, Elizabeth caught sight of the chart and the stack of unread magazines that awaited her.

"You can leave it by the door," Elizabeth said, returning to her desk. "I'll eat as soon as I get a chance." For the moment, nothing was more compelling than uncovering the great mystery unfolding before her.

"Barron, you look like hell," Matt said to himself. He studied his reflection in the mirror that hung in the entrance of Julia's lush apartment. In a matter of days, he seemed to have transformed into another person entirely. It was like looking through a crystal ball and seeing the person he was going to be in twenty years. And Matt didn't like what he saw.

Slowly, Matt pushed away a lock of limp hair that fell across his face. His fingertips touched his unshaven chin, tracing the outline of his newly grown beard and mustache. He had worn the same black jeans and white T-shirt for three days. Sweat and dirt permeated his clothes. Still, he had no intention of doing anything about it. *Nothing matters anymore,* he reminded himself.

What bothered him, more than anything, were the eyes. That's where the real change had taken place. Matt peered deeply into the reflection. The shining light in his amber eyes had disappeared, leaving them as dull, flat, and impenetrable as un-polished brass. They had the look of a man who'd witnessed pain and misery and wondered if there was any good left in the world.

"I made you a sandwich," a voice called from behind.

Matt looked up to see Bridget's reflection in the mirror. He turned around to face her. "Thanks."

"I left it in the fridge," she said, tying a dark brown scarf over her head. "I'll stop in tomorrow to see you. Will you be here?"

Matt scratched the bristles on his chin. "I'll probably be back at my place."

Bridget's eyes were downcast. "Do you need anything? Is there something I should bring?"

"No . . . no," Matt answered tiredly. He wrapped his arms around Bridget and embraced her warmly. "Thanks for coming by. I'd probably fall apart if you weren't around."

"You know exactly where I am if you need any-thing." Bridget kissed him on the cheek. "Please don't hesitate."

"Okay, and thanks again." Matt waved good-bye to her and closed the door. He turned around slowly, confronted for the first time by the cold hush of the marble hallway. He strained to re-member Julia's voice, to imagine her calling to him from another room. But he couldn't hear it. There was only silence.

*It's too soon.* Tears came to his swollen eyes. *I shouldn't be here—not yet.* Matt had wanted to wait before returning to Julia's apartment, but burning questions churned within him. And he wouldn't rest until he had some answers.

Matt's heavy black boots echoed as he made his way down the hallway to Julia's bedroom. *Did you really kill yourself, Julia?* It was a question that had haunted him every moment since that horrible day on the studio lot. *Was it something I did?*

His mind began to race as he approached Julia's desk. Papers were scattered across the top of the antique table. Matt's head throbbed as he sorted through them. Julia's appointment calendar, filled with meetings scheduled all through the summer, was laying open. Wedding arrangements were scribbled on various pieces of paper. Matt's pulse began to quicken, and his search became frantic as he hunted for a suicide note. He needed something—anything—that would explain why Julia was dead.

At last, he came across a letter. It was addressed to Julia's mother. Gingerly, Matt opened the envelope and took out the letter.

*Dear Mom,*

*Just a quick note to let you know that all the arrangements have been made for your visit. I'm so glad you're going to be here for the big day. I can't wait for you to meet Matt—he's such a wonderful man. I'm sure*

44

*you're going to love him. The only thing that could possibly make me happier would be if we were married right now. We have just a week to go, but it feels like forever.*

*See you soon.*
*Love,*
*Julia*

Julia had written the letter on the morning of the day she'd died.

Relief swept over Matt like a crashing wave. *She didn't kill herself.* He closed his eyes as the realization penetrated his brain. *It wasn't my fault.*

Matt reached for the phone on Julia's nightstand and quickly dialed the number for the district attorney. If Julia wasn't responsible for her own death, it was time to find out who was.

"District attorney's office," a voice said.

"Yes, this is Matt Barron. I would like to speak to the DA, please."

The line went quiet, then a deep voice came over the phone. "Stan Harris."

"Mr. Harris, this is Matt Barron." Matt gripped the receiver with both hands, as though it were a lifeline. "I'm calling about my girlfriend, Julia Reynolds."

"The suicide?"

"No—I mean, yes," Matt stammered. "What I mean is, everyone thinks it's a suicide, but I have proof that it wasn't."

The DA sighed loudly. "And what makes you think that?"

"I found a letter she wrote to her mother the day she died. She was saying how excited she was about getting married and . . . well, there's just no way she could've killed herself."

"Mr. Barron"—Stan Harris's voice was dry and flat—"people will surprise you. Are you sure you really knew your girlfriend?"

"Of course I did!" Matt felt the blood pounding in his brain. "All I'm saying is that you'll probably want to take a look at the letter for the investigation."

"That's very thoughtful of you, but there isn't going to be an investigation."

Matt's heart caught in his throat. "Why not?"

"It's a clear-cut case of suicide."

"But I'm telling you it's not!" Matt shouted into the phone.

The DA's voice remained calm. "There's no reason why I should waste taxpayers' money on an investigation when the conclusion is so obvious."

Matt inhaled deeply, fighting off the hot rage that was smoldering within. "Aren't you overlooking the possibility that it was an accident? Maybe the movie studio was negligent!"

"What are you planning to do? Sue for some big bucks?" The DA chuckled. "You think you're the only one this has happened to, but I'll let you in on a little secret: It happens to hundreds of people every day."

Matt felt his blood run cold. His fingers loosened, and the receiver started to slip through his fingers.

"It's the same old story every single time," Harris continued. "Loved ones often can't deal with the fact that a person didn't want to live."

"Are you guys ready?" Elizabeth called through the door of her dorm room.

"Are you kidding? I've waited two whole days for this!" Nina said excitedly.

"Hurry up, Liz," Jessica said, pounding on the door. "I miss my room."

Wearily, Elizabeth unbolted the door and yawned loudly. When she opened her eyes, she saw Tom, Nina, and Jessica staring back at her with anticipation.

Elizabeth held up the thirty-page paper in a blue binder, for all to see. "Behold—'The Suicide Paper.'"

"Looks impressive," Tom said as he watched Elizabeth yawn again. "Not bad for working two days straight."

Elizabeth leaned her head on Jessica's shoulder. "Thanks for staying with Isabella," she said to her twin.

"No problem," Jessica answered. "Besides, I heard you were talking aloud to your stuffed animals the whole time. I don't think I would've wanted to be around for that."

Elizabeth closed her eyes and giggled. "I get a

little strange when I don't get any sleep."

Nina jumped up and down excitedly, her braids clicking with each movement. "So tell us all about this exciting paper."

"It's not that exciting, really," Elizabeth said. Her stinging eyes began to water. "In fact, I think my whole theory is a bit far-fetched. I'd be embarrassed to tell you about it."

"You checked your facts and followed a logical argument, right?" Tom said as he snaked his arms around Elizabeth's waist.

"Yeah." Elizabeth smiled. She pressed her cheek against his.

"Then it can't be that far-fetched," Nina added.

"I don't know." Elizabeth yawned again. "Could one of you deliver that to Professor Zartman's office for me right away?"

Tom, Nina, and Jessica all nodded furiously.

"I think I should do it," Tom said casually as he took the paper from Elizabeth. "After all, I am the head journalist at WSVU. I know Professor Zartman pretty well."

Nina took the paper from Tom. "That's true, but let's not forget that I'm Elizabeth's best friend. It's my duty."

Jessica cleared her throat. "Ahem. As Elizabeth's twin sister, the job is obviously mine. If Liz can't be there, I'm the next best thing."

Elizabeth rolled her eyes. "Look, I don't care who goes. You can *all* go if you want."

Tom, Nina, and Jessica looked at one another excitedly.

"But you can't read it," Elizabeth added.

Their faces fell.

"Don't look at me like that!" she said at their pouting expressions. "I'll tell you all about it sometime. But right now, I've had enough of high-stakes Hollywood." Elizabeth turned off the light. "Now, if you'll excuse me, I'm going to crash."

# *Chapter Four*

"Hey there, buddy!" Bishop greeted John Shaw with a toothy grin.

Shaw was the head of Worldwide Publishing and a longtime gambling crony of Bishop's. Normally, Shaw carried an expression of detached amusement, but today, his face was flushed and his lips were drawn into a tight line.

"Are you heading down to the track early tonight?" Bishop asked.

"I think we'd all better cool it for a while," Shaw answered as he loosened his striped tie with one hand. The other hand held a blue folder.

Bishop leaned back in his chair. "Your blood pressure's rising again—I can tell," he said. "Maybe it's time you cut yourself loose from Worldwide Publishing and take up fishing, instead."

Shaw tossed the blue folder onto Bishop's desk. "I might not have any choice in the matter," he said grimly. He nodded toward the folder. "Take a look at that."

Several moments passed before Bishop finally reached for it. His eyes stayed focused on Shaw as Bishop dragged the folder across the glass top of his desk. He turned to the first page. "'The Suicide Paper' by Elizabeth Wakefield. What is this?"

"It's a whole lot of trouble for us, that's what." Worry lines creased Shaw's forehead. His voice suddenly dropped to a hoarse whisper. "That paper explains the entire murder plot!"

A shadow of suspicion darkened Bishop's features. "There's no way anyone could know about this." His voice was thick with accusation. "*I've* managed to keep things airtight."

"Look, I didn't leak it, if that's what you think." Shaw scratched the bald spot on the top of his head. "If anything, I averted disaster. You should be thanking me." He walked over to the window and looked out over the Hollywood hills. "I stopped by the *Hollywood Daily,* and my senior editor, Kate Morgan, handed me that folder. She wanted to run the story, but I made her pull it. I told her I couldn't run it because you were a good friend of mine."

"So where'd she get it?"

Shaw took off his wire-rimmed glasses and wiped the lenses with a handkerchief. "Kate mentioned something about a friend of hers, a Professor Cynthia Zartman. She teaches at Sweet

Valley University. It seems that one of Zartman's students handed that paper in to her."

Bishop squinted and let out a booming laugh. "You're trying to tell me that some college kid came up with this on her own? How stupid do you think I am?"

Shaw put his glasses back on and tucked the handkerchief in his back pocket. "I don't believe it, either. I think someone put her up to it." He swallowed hard. "I'm just glad I intercepted it."

"Don't worry about a thing," Bishop said coolly. "I've got the law-enforcement side covered. I talked to Dawson earlier, and he agreed to call off the investigation. By the way, George sends his regards."

Shaw's face turned a deeper shade. "Is that going to be enough to keep the cover on it?"

"I expect you to keep the publishing side clear."

"It w-won't be good enough," Shaw stammered. "People have read 'The Suicide Paper.' There's bound to be talk." His eyes darted wildly around the room. "If this thing gets out about you and Mammoth Pictures, everyone's bound to find out about your gambling connection to Dawson and McKenna. It's going to be over for us."

Bishop sneered. "In case you've forgotten, I'm the one with the most to lose. I appreciate your concern," he answered flatly.

"I'm sorry . . . you know how it is. . . ."

Bishop picked up the phone. "Pierce, get in my office right now!" The same moment he slammed the receiver down, Pierce came bounding through the door.

"Don't worry about a thing, Mr. Shaw," Bishop said to his red-faced friend. "I'm going to take care of the situation right now."

"Elizabeth! Come on in!" Professor Zartman smiled warmly as she took a seat behind the desk of her cluttered office. "I left the message for you barely five minutes ago. You certainly didn't waste any time."

"I had a free moment, so I thought I'd come over," Elizabeth said, her faced flushed from the run across campus. She was carrying a large cardboard box, and as she tried to squeeze through the narrow doorway, Elizabeth accidentally ran into the corner of a filing cabinet.

"Ow!" she yelped.

"Be careful!" Professor Zartman said. "Are you all right?"

"I'm fine," Elizabeth answered as she dropped the crumpled box on the floor. "I'm not so sure about this box, though."

"What's in there?" Zartman moved a stack of student papers from a chair to the bookshelf over her desk.

Elizabeth took a seat in the empty chair. "I don't know. It was sitting outside your office, so I thought I'd bring it in for you."

"I don't remember ordering anything. . . ." Zartman closed her brown eyes and rubbed her temples, as if she were probing the recesses of her brain. "But then again, I'm so disorganized, it's very possible that I've just forgotten."

Elizabeth ran a finger over the dent in the cardboard. "I hope it wasn't anything too valuable."

Zartman shook her head. "It's probably just books or papers." She cleared a spot on her desk and placed the pile of papers on the floor near the filing cabinet, alongside many other stacks. Zartman stared at the heaps with disgust, as though they were a fungus that was slowly taking over the office. "As if I need *more* paper."

A light, fluttering feeling of anticipation came over Elizabeth as she watched the professor rearranging her office. *Why does she want to see me?* she wondered to herself. On the way over, her mind had whirled with possibilities. *Maybe she wants to tell me that she liked my paper . . . or that she wants to hire me as a teaching assistant . . . or maybe she knows of a summer job working at a newspaper and she thinks I'd be perfect for* it. . . .

But now, as she sat in the office and the professor scurried busily around her, Elizabeth wondered if maybe she had overreacted a bit. Professor Zartman seemed far too preoccupied to have any important news.

"You seem really busy," Elizabeth said casually. She slung her blue backpack over her shoulder. "Maybe I should come back another time."

"No, please stay." Zartman set the cardboard

box on top of her cleared desk and reached for a pair of scissors. "I wanted to talk to you about your paper."

Elizabeth's stomach did a somersault. She slipped the backpack off her shoulder and put it on the floor while she patiently waited for Zartman to continue.

"This is odd," the professor said as she stared at the label on the box. "There's no return address." She shrugged and cut through the package twine with the scissors. "Anyway, back to 'The Suicide Paper.' I wanted to tell you that you did a fantastic job."

"Thanks," Elizabeth answered humbly. A warm glow of satisfaction washed over her, like the California sun on a perfect summer day. "I was afraid it might seem a bit far-fetched."

"Well, it is quite an outlandish theory," Zartman said as she pulled off a bit of packing tape. "Especially to implicate the CEO of Mammoth Pictures in Julia Reynolds's death. But your theory was well supported, and that's what makes for real journalism." She turned to Elizabeth and smiled. Her face was soft and youthful. "Not to mention the enormous amount of time and effort you put into what was supposed to be a short assignment."

Elizabeth looked down at her hands, folded neatly in her lap. "It was a lot of fun. I think I've discovered that I'm meant to be an investigative reporter.".

Zartman put down the scissors. "I think you

are, too." She nodded. "But there's still so much you need to learn about the business."

"I know," Elizabeth admitted. She looked with envy at the numerous framed newspaper articles that lined the walls of the office. All of them had been written by Professor Zartman. "I'm all ready to begin my career. I just don't know how to get started."

"What about submitting 'The Suicide Paper' to a big newspaper?"

Elizabeth drew in a quick breath. "I'm not sure I could do that. . . ."

"I had a feeling you might be a bit shy about it," Professor Zartman said sheepishly as she resumed opening the cardboard box. "That's why I did it for you."

"What?" Elizabeth felt her solar plexus dissolving.

The tape made a loud ripping sound as Zartman tore it off the box. "Kate Morgan, my roommate from college, works for the *Hollywood Daily*. I sent your paper over for her to look at." The professor wadded the tape into a ball and tossed it into the trash can next to her desk. "The last time I spoke to Kate, she seemed really interested in running it. The only thing she had to do was to okay it with her boss." She smiled optimistically. "We should have an answer soon."

A lightning bolt of excitement shot straight through Elizabeth. "I can't believe it," she said breathlessly.

"I hope you don't mind."

"Not at all," she gushed. "It would be so incredible to see my name in print."

Strong afternoon sunlight poured in, illuminating the tiny, drab office. "It *would* be terrific, and it would help you get your foot in the door for a job at a real newspaper." Professor Zartman stopped unwrapping for a moment, her smile fading. "But don't get too excited. We don't know yet if Kate is going to run the story. And even if you publish a hundred stories, I guarantee your first job will be getting coffee for some stressed-out editor," she said evenly. "People in journalism are funny that way: They expect you to work your way up from the bottom."

"I can respect that," Elizabeth answered. Her blue-green eyes sparkled in the sunlight like the waters of the Pacific. "You have to pay your dues."

"Good. I'm glad you see it that way," Zartman said, turning back to the package. A slow grin played at the corners of her mouth. "So if you don't mind, how would you like to start practicing for your first job?"

Elizabeth jumped to her feet. "How do you take your coffee?" she said with a laugh.

"Today, I need it as black as possible," Zartman sighed. She pulled back one of the box flaps. "Thanks a lot, Liz."

"I'll be back in a sec," Elizabeth said before bounding down to the end of the hallway, where the coffeemaker was.

*I can't believe it*, Elizabeth thought ecstatically. *The* Hollywood Daily *might print my paper!* All the hard work had definitely paid off. But Elizabeth owed it all to Professor Zartman. If she hadn't submitted the paper to Kate Morgan, none of this would've happened.

Elizabeth reached for the coffeepot, when suddenly a thunderous noise shook the floor beneath her. In a fraction of a second she turned around to see a ball of white-hot fire burst from the doorway of Professor Zartman's office.

*"Oh no!"* Elizabeth shrieked in horror as the force of the explosion hurled her against the wall.


"Mr. Barron, this is Roger Perry from *The Roger Perry Show*. I'd like to talk to you about making an appearance on my program sometime next week. We're doing a piece called 'Hot Celebrities Who Have Lost Their Fiancées to Suicide.' I think it will be a very rewarding experience for you. Please call me at 555-7883. Thanks."

The answering machine stopped recording.

Matt kicked aside a few empty take-out containers and propped his bare feet on top of the glass coffee-table aquarium that sat in the middle of his living room. Through the glass top, he watched the yellow and orange tropical fish glide gracefully from one side of the aquarium to the other.

"You guys have it easy," Matt said to the fish, his voice flat and emotionless. "All you have to worry about is what you're going to eat and where you're going to swim to next." The fish continued to sail through the water, unaffected by Matt's words. "You'll never know what it's like to lose someone."

The phone rang.

Matt leaned back. His eyes were hot and itchy from a lack of sleep. His white T-shirt was covered with pizza sauce from two days before. Bridget had been nice enough to bring his clothes to the cleaners, but Matt didn't have the energy to change. Instead, the clean clothes were piled at one end of the couch, untouched. Matt would sometimes use them as a pillow whenever he managed to drift off to sleep for a few minutes.

*Ring. Ring.*

"Another insane journalist," Matt mumbled to one of the Cardinal Tetras that was feeding in the corner of the aquarium. He made no move to pick up the phone, but waited instead for the answering machine to turn on.

*Beep.*

"Hi, Mr. Barron, this is Kate Morgan speaking. I don't know if you're familiar with my work—I'm a reporter with the *Hollywood Daily* . . ."

"Good for you, Kate Morgan," Matt said sarcastically to the answering machine as he reclined on the couch.

"I just wanted you to know that I don't believe Julia killed herself. I think it's all much more complicated than anyone's willing to admit. I have a few theories of my own. . . ."

Matt's golden eyes widened. He jumped over the back of the couch and grabbed the receiver. "Hello?" he said into the phone. "This is Matt."

"I'm so glad you picked up the phone," Kate answered. "I know this is a bad time for you, but we can't let this go."

Blood rushed through his body. "What do you know about Julia?"

"I don't *know* anything," Kate whispered. "But something came across my desk that could explain the whole mystery. My boss won't let me run it, but I think you'd be interested in hearing the details."

"What is it?" Matt said desperately. The answers he had been waiting for loomed in the distance, like a ray of daylight at the end of an underground tunnel. "I need to know."

"I'm sorry, but it's nothing I can get into over the phone," Kate said in a hushed voice. "Can you meet me tomorrow?"

Pierce leaned against the side of the telephone booth to steady his nerves. The booth was outside, in the back corner of the *Hollywood Daily* employee parking lot. It was midafternoon, and the lot was full of cars, but there were very few people around. Everyone was inside, taking refuge from the sweltering heat of the sun. Despite the eighty-degree temperature, Pierce's teeth began to chatter.

*You don't have to do this,* Pierce told himself as

he zipped up the front of his blue windbreaker. He knew that in the extreme heat the jacket made him look suspicious, but he couldn't think of any other way to do it. The suffocating material was like an incubator, drenching Pierce's body in sweat.

The young woman in the phone booth, whom Pierce assumed was Kate Morgan, poked her head out and smiled at him. "I have just one more call to make, then I'll be done. Okay?" she said.

Pierce nodded imperceptibly. *She seems nice,* he thought miserably. *Is she married? Does she have many friends? Any children?* He craved to know every little detail of her life. But it was best if he knew nothing.

Yet, the questions remained. *How could this person possibly be a threat to Mammoth Pictures?*

*"She knows too much."*

That's what Bishop had said yesterday when he had called Pierce into his office. It was right after John Shaw had left, looking pale and shaken.

"I have another job for you," Bishop had said.

Pierce had felt his knees buckle underneath him, and he'd clutched the corner of Bishop's desk to keep from falling over. "What kind of job?" he'd asked weakly.

"Same as the one you did out on the studio lot." Bishop had wiped his forehead with a red silk handkerchief and shoved it into the pocket of his suit jacket. "Only this time it's a college professor."

"This is crazy—"

"You won't have any direct contact this time," Bishop had forcefully interrupted. "I have a friend who's making up a package for Professor Zartman, and all you need to do is deliver it."

Pierce remembered how his knuckles had turned white as he'd gripped the edge of the desk. "What kind of package?"

Bishop's fat, purple lips had pouted slightly. "A surprise package," he had answered. "Don't worry about it. Your only concern is making sure she gets it."

"But why her? What has she done?" Pierce had pleaded.

Bishop had stuck an unlit cigar in the corner of his mouth. "She knows too much," he'd said. "And believe me, you want her to keep quiet as much as I do."

As Pierce waited outside of the phone booth, he wished he'd been more forceful with Bishop. He should've walked out.

*I wonder if the professor's found the package by now.* Pierce glanced anxiously at his watch. The thought of the professor opening the package bomb sickened him, but in a detached way. It was like reading about some horrible story in the newspaper. Pierce had nothing against the professor, had never met her, and wasn't the person who'd constructed the bomb. He'd only delivered it.

*It's not my fault.*

Pierce pressed his aching head against the glass of the telephone booth. He heard the low murmur of the woman's conversation, but couldn't make out any of the words. Thoughts pounded through his brain in rapid succession.

*I didn't kill Julia, either. . . . I just told her when to jump. If she had looked, she would've seen it was a bad time. It's not my fault. . . .*

Just a few hours ago, McKenna had come barging into Pierce's office to give him the next assignment. Kate Morgan.

"There's a journalist we need you to take care of," McKenna had said. He'd handed Pierce a large yellow envelope—inside was a gun. "It's easy," McKenna had said. "All you have to do is pull the trigger."

Pierce scanned the parking lot. No one was in sight. With trembling fingers, he reached into his jacket pocket and felt the cold barrel of the .45 magnum.

*How many others know too much?* He closed his watery eyes and imagined the desolation of a prison cell. That's where he'd spend the rest of his life if the scandal broke. Bitter acid stung his throat. *I'm not going to jail for you, Bishop.*

"Sorry that took so long," the woman said cheerfully as she stepped out of the booth. The sun played upon her short ash-blond hair. "It's all yours now."

Pierce glared at her through glassy eyes. "Are you Kate Morgan?" he asked. The damp jacket clung to his skin.

63

"Yes," she answered. Her dark eyes narrowed. "Can I help you with something?"

A crushing guilt seized Pierce, strangling him in its overpowering claws. *Save me from this,* he pleaded silently to her kind face. *Help me get out of this mess.* His fingers traced the outline of the gun for a second time. The sensation of the smooth metal against his skin made Pierce's stomach heave.

"Are you all right?" Kate asked.

Pierce clutched his abdomen and doubled over in pain. His stomach muscles contracted in violent spasms.

*"She knows too much"* . . . Bishop's words turned over again and again in his frantic mind. *"She knows too much."*

Kate looked scared. "Is there anything you need?"

Then, with a whisper-light touch, she placed a compassionate hand on Pierce's shoulder.

Kate's tenderness drove deeply into Pierce, like a knife slicing through his heart. It penetrated the murky darkness that had invaded him in the last few days, unleashing dragons of hopelessness and terror. Kate filled Pierce with longing for the person he once was, and loathing for the person he had become.

"No!" he screamed painfully, backing away from her.

"Do you need a doctor?" Kate anxiously stepped back into the phone booth. "I'm going to call a doctor—"

As he watched her dial the number, Pierce slid his hand into the front pocket of his jacket. Tears poured freely from his eyes. Slowly, he drew the gun. Without any hesitation, he pressed the barrel against the back of Kate's head and pulled the trigger.

# Chapter Five

"How much longer is it going to take to edit the footage of the ballet concert?" Tom looked nervously at the clock on the wall of the WSVU studio. They only had two hours before airtime, and at least three stories still had to be put together, or there wouldn't be enough to fill the broadcast.

Zachary Warren, a WSVU reporter, stared diligently at the four TV monitors in front of him. "I need about forty minutes," he said, rolling up his sleeves. "But its going to take another hour to write the copy and do the voice-overs."

Tom made a mad dash for the computer station by the window. "I'll tell you what—I'll write the copy, you finish the editing," he delegated. "Where are your notes?"

Zack tossed a red notebook in Tom's direction. "Everything's in there."

Tom scanned the notebook pages and began

typing away. "At this rate, we'll be lucky to get two stories done," he said over his shoulder. "I hope Elizabeth is in the mood to improvise on the air tonight."

"Where is Elizabeth, anyway?" Zack asked. "We could really use her help."

"She had a meeting with Professor Zartman." Tom continued typing as he spoke, hardly missing a beat. "She's supposed to come right over afterward. We can have her do the voice-overs."

"Good," Zack said as he rewound the videotape. "My timing's always off."

*I know exactly what you mean,* Tom thought gloomily. That's how he'd describe his relationship with Elizabeth lately—they couldn't coordinate anything. Ever since Elizabeth had spent two days working on her journalism paper, Tom had barely been able to spend any time with her. If he didn't have stories of his own to cover, she was running off to class. If she wasn't busy with friends, he had exams to study for. The only real time they'd spent with each other was in the station, where they were too busy making deadlines to even have a decent conversation.

"Do you have any exciting plans for tonight?" Zack asked.

Tom continued typing furiously on the keyboard. "I don't have any classes tomorrow, so I'm hoping Elizabeth will want to go out to dinner or catch a movie. That is, if she isn't too busy."

"I know how that is. I've been so crazy here at

the station that I haven't seen my girlfriend once this week."

"Hey, Zack, I'm sorry about that." Tom stopped typing and turned his chair around. "If you want some time off, just say the word."

"No, it's okay," Zack said honestly. "I don't mind coming in, and besides, you need all the help you can get." He pressed the fast-forward button, and the ballerina on the TV screen twirled out of control. "What I don't understand is, why do you have to do a broadcast every single night? It would be so much easier if we could just knock it down to three nights a week."

Tom rolled his head from side to side, trying to release the tension in his neck muscles. "The faculty won't let us do it," he said. "All the journalism professors want a nightly campus news show. Apparently, it's a bigger draw for potential journalism students who are thinking about enrolling at SVU. If you ask me, it sounds like a ploy for the English department to get more money."

"I've got an idea." Zack flashed Tom an evil grin. "Why don't we just blow up the studio—or better yet, blow up the English department. Then we could make up our own rules and broadcast when we feel like it."

Tom laughed. "Think of the weird stor—" A loud rumbling noise and the sound of breaking glass stopped Tom mid-sentence. Looking out the window, he caught sight of thick black smoke and orange flames shooting out of a third-story window in the English building.

"Whoa, Zack," Tom muttered. "What did you do?"

Zack's eyes bulged. "Nothing, I swear—it was just a joke!" The smoke became heavier as the fire intensified. "It looks like Professor Zartman's office. Didn't you say Elizabeth was over there?"

Tom didn't answer. He ran out the door.

"Professor Zartman!" Elizabeth screamed as she lay on the floor by the coffeemaker. The hallway was saturated with soot and smoke, making the air as black as night.

Blinded by the stinging fumes, Elizabeth listened for sounds from Zartman's office. She couldn't hear any movement, only the crackling sizzle of flames devouring the office. "Can you hear me?" Elizabeth yelled in panic. "Are you okay?"

The fire alarm sounded, its screech pulsating in Elizabeth's ears. *I have to get out of here,* she thought in panic.

Every nerve on edge, Elizabeth felt the floor with her bare hands. Broken glass from the shattered coffeepot surrounded her. Slowly, she crawled on her hands and knees, staying below the billowing smoke. Tears stung Elizabeth's eyes as the glass shards drove deep into the palms of her hands. "Somebody help me!" she cried out in pain.

But her voice was drowned out by the wail of the alarm.

Elizabeth inched down the hallway, staying close to the wall, relying solely on her sense of touch to guide her. In her mind's eye, she pictured the corridor.

*Zartman's office is only four doors away,* Elizabeth remembered. Two doors beyond that was the emergency exit. She held her breath and continued on.

*Keep going. You're almost there,* an inner voice guided her as her hands felt for the molding of the second doorway. The smoke became heavier as Elizabeth neared Zartman's office, and she strained, trying to hold her breath. Waves of heat from the fire blasted against her face. *Hold on, just a little longer . . .* Her chest seemed to be collapsing as her lungs craved fresh air. At last, her body's reflexes won out, and Elizabeth inhaled deeply of the blackened atmosphere.

"Help," she wheezed. But no one seemed to hear. The smoke entered her system rapidly, pricking like hot needles as it traveled through her esophagus and into her lungs. Elizabeth coughed violently. Suddenly her head felt light, as if she had been turned upside down. Disorientation seized Elizabeth, destroying her sense of direction. It was like being hurled into outer space, never knowing which way is up.

"Help me!" Elizabeth cried out again. She stopped for a moment, uncertain of which direction to take. *Where's the exit?* she thought hysterically. *Take a left,* instinct told her. But rationality kept her frozen in place, with fear of pushing deeper into the inferno.

*I don't want to die.*

Terror and loneliness descended upon her like blazing birds of prey. She would die alone, consumed by the fire that raged in Zartman's office only one door away. *I'm never going to get out of here.* Elizabeth slumped against the scorching wall.

As she fell backward, the wall gave way. It was a door. The motion sent Elizabeth tumbling onto the carpet of one of the faculty offices. A burst of clean air flooded her lungs. Elizabeth's burning eyes looked up to see a sliver of sunlight, just before clouds of black smoke engulfed the room.

"I can't believe she's dead!" Jessica cried. Tears streamed down her face. "She meant the world to me. She must've meant a lot to you, too."

"She was everything," the stranger answered hoarsely.

Jessica wiped away a fresh tear and placed the bouquet of red orchids in front of Julia Reynolds's gravestone. In the week since her death, dozens of floral arrangements had been left there. Judging from the messages written on the cards, Jessica figured that many of the bouquets were from admiring fans.

Jessica pulled a tissue from the pocket of her jeans and blew her nose loudly. "Sorry," she said to the stranger standing beside her. He was a man in his early thirties with a weary face and a sad demeanor.

71

For some reason, Jessica felt a strange kinship to him. "I didn't plan on freaking out like this. But seeing her name on the headstone makes it all so . . . final." She brushed the back of her hand across her swollen cheek. "It's weird how I never got to meet her when she was alive . . . and now, here I am."

"She was a beautiful person," the stranger said.

*Who is this guy?* Jessica wondered silently. *Did he know Julia?* Out of the corner of her eye, Jessica made a quick assessment of the stranger's appearance: dirty T-shirt, old jeans, cowboy boots, scraggly beard. The summer wind changed direction, and Jessica's nose told her that the man hadn't washed in days. *There's no way . . . ,* she decided instantly. Julia had been a star, surrounding herself with wealthy, sophisticated, successful people who took frequent baths. This man was obviously just a distraught fan.

"Now that she's gone, there's nothing left." He began to sob. His shoulders shook as he took in deep, mournful breaths. "There's nothing left," he repeated.

Jessica whipped out a fresh tissue and handed it to him. "Don't say things like that," she said gently. "Life has to keep on going for the rest of us."

The stranger shook his head. "It's all over for me. It ended the day she died."

"I was really upset, too, when I heard the news." Jessica placed a sympathetic hand on his shoulder. Worry lines creased her forehead. *This guy's really going off the deep end,* she thought to herself. *What if he does something crazy? What if he tries to hurt himself?* "I know what you're thinking—don't do it."

"Don't do what?"

"Don't kill yourself!" Jessica said emphatically. "It's not worth it. Life is pretty tough right now, but it'll get easier. Think of how upset Julia would be if she knew you were going to end it all because of her."

The man lifted his head and stared at Jessica. For the first time, she became aware of his startlingly handsome face. His golden eyes held her gaze. Their depths held secrets of love and loss and unending pain. One moment, they lured her in; the next, they shut her out completely.

Jessica flinchingly pulled her hand away from his shoulder, as though it had been burned by a flame. "I'm so sorry," she whispered.

The stranger turned around and started down the path to the entrance of the cemetery. His head bowed down, he continued on without looking back.

Elizabeth clutched her throat as the coughing grew worse. *If only this were all just a horrible dream.* But it wasn't. Ominous charcoal clouds towered over her, while deadly flames spread in every direction.

"Here, have some water," one of the paramedics said, handing Elizabeth a cup. He wrapped a thermal blanket around her shoulders. "You should move back a little to the grassy area. You're too close to the building."

Elizabeth took a sip of water. The cooling liquid temporarily eased the stinging in her throat. "Thanks," she said as she watched two firefighters climb the extension ladder up to the third floor. Hundreds of people had gathered in the quad to watch the blaze.

"Are you okay for now? Do you need anything else?" the paramedic asked.

Elizabeth shook her head. "I'm fine."

"The emergency staff will come by to take a look at you as soon as they can," he said, before running back to the ambulance.

Gingerly, she pulled the thermal blanket around herself for comfort. Elizabeth struggled to understand the chaos around her, to absorb the details of what had just taken place. It had all happened in a flash—one minute she was talking to her favorite professor, the next minute . . .

"There you are. Thank goodness you're all right."

Elizabeth smiled weakly at Tom, whose brown eyes reflected the same mixture of horror and relief that she was feeling. He drew her close, kissing her softly on the lips.

"I saw the smoke from WSVU . . ." Tom's voice faltered. "What happened?"

Fresh tears came to her eyes. "I'm not sure. The police think someone sent Professor Zartman a package bomb." Elizabeth broke down. She rested her head limply against his strong shoulder. "I found that package outside her door. I carried it inside for her. She started to unwrap it, then she sent me in the hallway to get her some coffee. That's when I saw the explosion."

Tom swallowed hard. "Did she survive?"

Elizabeth buried her face in Tom's neck. "The detective I spoke with said she was killed instantly." Her body trembled. "She was such a wonderful person, Tom. Why would somebody want to kill her?"

A man in a dark gray suit and blue tie walked over to where they were sitting. "Sorry to interrupt—," he said in an official voice. He pulled a shiny badge from his pocket and flashed it at them. "I'm Detective Curtis. I just need to ask you a few questions."

Elizabeth pulled away from Tom and cleared her throat. "What do you need to know?" she asked tiredly.

"You were the student who was with Cynthia Zartman just before the explosion, is that correct?" Detective Curtis flipped open a notepad and jotted down a few notes with a pencil.

"Yes. My name is Elizabeth Wakefield."

"Ms. Wakefield, where were you at the exact moment the explosion took place?"

"At the end of the hallway. I was getting Professor Zartman some coffee."

"And what did you do?"

"I called out for her, but there was no answer,"

Elizabeth said. "The smoke was so thick that I couldn't see anything. So I crawled on my hands and knees toward her office."

The detective pushed the bridge of his sunglasses higher up on his nose. "Did you see or hear anything unusual?"

"Like I said, I couldn't see or hear anything," she answered impatiently.

Detective Curtis pressed on. "How did you get out of the building?"

"I found an office door that was open," Elizabeth said. "I crawled out the window and onto the fire escape." She rubbed her temples, hoping to ease the throbbing in her head. "Are all these questions really necessary? I already gave my statement to Detective Marsh."

The detective stopped writing. "Who?"

"*Detective Marsh*," she enunciated, the agitation increasing in her voice. "He's tall and lanky. He was standing over there by the ambulance." She looked in the direction of the medical crew, but he was nowhere in sight. "I don't see him now."

"I'm sorry, Ms. Wakefield, you must be confused." Detective Curtis closed his notebook. "We don't have anyone in the department by that name."

# Chapter
## Six

"Did you get *any* sleep last night?" Jessica asked. She pushed back the purple satin comforter on her bed and propped herself up on her elbows.

On the other side of the room, Elizabeth sat at her desk, still wearing her pink-and-white-striped pajamas. Her head rested on the desktop. "I guess I must've dozed off once or twice," she said numbly.

Jessica combed through the tangles in her hair with her fingers. "You just went through an incredibly traumatic experience. It might be a while before you have a full night's sleep."

Elizabeth lifted her head groggily. "It's not like I'm not tired enough. It's just that my mind won't stop going."

Jessica nodded knowingly. "I was the exact same way after James Montgomery attacked me at Lookout Point. I kept reliving that night over and over again in my mind."

"The events leading up to the explosion don't bother me as much as what happened after." Elizabeth moved away from her desk and sat down on the edge of Jessica's bed. "That whole thing about Detective Marsh questioning me, then finding out that there isn't anyone in the department with that name—" She shuddered. "The whole thing gives me a bad feeling."

"Maybe you were just confused, like Detective Curtis said."

"No," Elizabeth answered firmly. "The more I think about it, the more certain I am that something weird is going on. When I thought it over last night, I remembered that the guy who had claimed to be Detective Marsh never showed me his badge. I should've asked to see some identification, but I was so out of it that I wasn't paying attention."

Jessica puckered her lips thoughtfully. "Did he do anything else that was weird?"

"I don't remember seeing him anywhere near the police cars. He hung out by the ambulance," she said. "And he seemed to be in a hurry. When Detective Curtis was questioning me, he took his time." Elizabeth held her head in her hands. "How could I be so stupid, Jess? It's so obvious now that he was impersonating a police officer!"

Jessica placed a reassuring hand on her sister's shoulder. "You were in shock. Your mind was on other things," she said sympathetically. "Do they have any idea who's responsible?"

"*They* don't," Elizabeth said through clenched teeth, "But *I'm* going to find out."

Morning sunlight streamed in through the window as Jessica raised the blinds. "Zartman was a well-respected teacher. I can't imagine that anyone would want to kill her." Jessica frowned. "Have you thought that maybe this is just a horrible, random thing?"

Elizabeth pulled a telephone book off the shelf and started flipping through the yellow pages. "I can't think that way—not until I've exhausted all the possibilities." She picked up the phone.

"Who are you calling?"

"Someone who might have a few answers," Elizabeth replied.

Jessica slipped on her purple satin robe and watched as her twin punched a number into the keypad. *Here she goes again,* Jessica thought grimly. Whenever there was a mystery that needed to be solved, Elizabeth was on the case. It wasn't enough that the authorities were stumped; Elizabeth always believed she could uncover something they may have overlooked.

"Yes, this is Elizabeth Wakefield. I need to speak to Kate Morgan," she said into the receiver. "She's considering one of my stories. It's urgent that I speak with her."

There was a brief moment of silence as Elizabeth listened to the person at the other end. Her brow was wrinkled, and her eyes held a look of fierce determination. Jessica pitied anyone who got in her sister's way.

"You don't understand—" Elizabeth's voice grew even more forceful. "It concerns her friend Cynthia Zartman."

There was another pause. Then Elizabeth's face took on a ghostly pallor. Sensing something was wrong, Jessica rushed to her side.

"What is it?" Jessica whispered.

The phone slipped out of Elizabeth's grasp and crashed to the floor. She turned, her lips pale and trembling. "Kate Morgan is dead."

"I want to speak with Detective Curtis, *now*!" Elizabeth shouted at the woman behind the counter at the police station. "This is an emergency!"

The young woman with dark curls shot Elizabeth a look of bored annoyance. "In this place, everything's an emergency," she said evenly as she slid a clipboard across the countertop. "Fill out the bottom section, then take a seat over there." She pointed to a cluster of orange vinyl chairs in the corner of the room. "Here's a pen," she said with a plastic smile.

Elizabeth pushed the clipboard aside. Her head throbbed with tension. "I'm not going to wait," she snapped. "If you don't bring Detective Curtis out here in two minutes, I'm going to report you!"

The woman behind the counter grinned, apparently unfazed by the threat. "Listen, ma'am.

Detective Curtis is on vacation in Hawaii. If you'll wait patiently, someone will be along to help you as soon as possible."

Elizabeth stormed over to the corner of the room and took a seat on a sticky vinyl chair. "How do you like that?" Elizabeth muttered under her breath. "One day Curtis is investigating a murder case, the next day he's island-hopping." Meanwhile, someone else had been murdered. Someone who was connected to Professor Zartman. Judging from the way the whole situation was being handled, Elizabeth had a nagging feeling that the case just might simply fall through the system's cracks.

"Ms. Wakefield, come right in." A pleasant-looking man with wavy blond hair and a cleft chin stepped out of a nearby office and motioned for her to come over.

Elizabeth smiled with relief. *Finally, a reasonable person I can talk to,* she said to herself as she approached the man.

"I'm Police Chief Nichols," he said, extending his hand. "Why don't you have a seat, and we can talk about what's troubling you."

Elizabeth shook his hand gratefully and sat in the folding chair near Chief Nichols's metal desk. Several engraved plaques decorated the walls of his small office.

"I came to speak with Detective Curtis, but I heard he was on vacation," she said.

"He left this morning." The sleeves of Chief Nichols's blue dress shirt were rolled up to the elbows, and his silver watchband gleamed under the harsh fluorescent lights. "So, how may I be of help to you?"

Elizabeth's headache began to subside. "I was in the explosion yesterday at Sweet Valley University. My professor, Cynthia Zartman, was killed."

"I'm sorry to hear that, Elizabeth," he said with a sympathetic tone. "You're a very lucky young woman to have survived."

"Yes, I know," she answered, looking down at her sneakered feet. "But I'm concerned that Professor Zartman's murderer won't be found."

Chief Nichols nodded in agreement. "I know what you mean. Unfortunately, in these violent times, random crimes are happening more and more frequently."

"But that's just it, " Elizabeth cut in. "I don't think it *was* random. I called one of Professor Zartman's colleagues this morning, and I found out that she'd been murdered yesterday in Hollywood."

The police chief's hazel eyes narrowed. "Another package bomb?"

"No. She was shot through the head in a parking lot outside her office."

"That's the answer, right there," Chief Nichols said, throwing his hands up in the air. "There's no connection. A serial murderer almost always picks one method and sticks with it."

Hot blood rushed to Elizabeth's face. "With all due respect, sir, I don't think you should be so quick to write it off," she said flatly. "Two women who knew each other died on the same day. They have to be connected somehow."

"Or maybe it's just a tragic coincidence," Nichols added. He laced his fingers behind his head and pensively stared at the white ceiling. "What sort of connection did you have in mind?"

"I don't know," Elizabeth admitted. She thought back to her conversation with Zartman. "Professor Zartman did mention that she and Kate were once college roommates. They have a history together."

Chief Nichols pressed a thick finger against his lips, as if he were trying to contain his laughter. He sat up straight in his chair, and Elizabeth sensed he was about to show her the door. "Is there anything else, Ms. Wakefield?"

*Think! This could be your only chance.* Elizabeth racked her brain, trying to think of any small detail that could link the two murders. The pressure she'd felt earlier returned, pounding repeatedly in her head. *Think . . . they were good friends . . . both journalists . . . they kept in touch . . .*

"If that's all, I'd like to thank you for coming in," Chief Nichols said cordially. He stood up. "Drop by when you have some free time, and I can give you a tour of the station."

*They lived fairly close to each other . . .* Elizabeth stood up to leave, when suddenly the answer came to her. *They both read the paper.*

"No wait!" she shouted. "It's my paper."

A puzzled expression twisted Chief Nichols's features. "What paper is that?"

Elizabeth's pulse quickened. It had to be the answer. "I wrote a paper about Julia Reynolds's death, and how it wasn't a suicide, but a conspiracy in the movie industry."

"A conspiracy theory?"

"From the research I had done, I came to the conclusion that she'd been murdered." Elizabeth spoke quickly. "Zartman liked it enough to send it to her friend Kate Morgan to look at. Before the explosion, Zartman told me that Kate wanted to publish it in the *Hollywood Daily*."

"Whoa, back up a second." Chief Nichols folded his arms across his chest. "Are you telling me that you think your paper is indirectly responsible for yesterday's murders?"

The muscles in Elizabeth's shoulders tensed, and the pressure of her headache intensified. "It's so obvious," she said. "The people who are involved in Julia's murder must've gotten wind of it, so they decided to get rid of everyone who saw the paper to keep them quiet." An icy chill ran down Elizabeth's spine. "I guess that means I'm next."

"I'm sure you worked very hard and that it was well written, but this idea that your little college paper has turned Hollywood on its head is a bit much." He chuckled. "Instead of journalism, maybe you should think about writing best-sellers. You'll probably make a lot more money."

Elizabeth's shoulders slumped in defeat. The

energy she'd had when she'd come in was suddenly drained from her. "Don't you think you should at least check it out? We can't let the killer get away with it."

"Both cases are in good hands, Ms. Wakefield," Chief Nichols said as he opened the door. "You can be certain that both killers will be brought to justice. You take care now."

"Oh, just one more thing before I go—"

The police chief's mouth was drawn up in a tight smile, and Elizabeth could tell that his patience had been stretched very near the breaking point. "Yes?"

"Could I use your phone? It's a local call."

Nichols motioned to the black phone on his desk. "Dial nine first."

Elizabeth dialed Nina's number with a trembling finger. They were supposed to meet for lunch as soon as Elizabeth returned to campus. Too many crazy things had happened in the last twenty-four hours, and she needed the familiar comfort of having lunch with her best friend. Maybe it would help clear her head.

The answering machine message came on, followed by the usual beep. "Nina, it's Liz. I need to see you right away. I'm at the police station now. I should be back to campus in about twenty minutes, so let's meet in the Coffee House in about half an hour. See you then."

Chief Nichols held the door open. "All set now?"

Elizabeth nodded. "Thanks for your help." *Or lack of it.*

She walked out into the hallway, and Chief Nichols's door closed behind her with a loud *slam*. Elizabeth passed the lobby with her head held high, careful not to meet the gaze of the woman behind the counter.

As soon as she reached the front steps, Elizabeth grabbed the railing to support herself. *What's wrong with me?* she wondered. *Why am I so paranoid?* Her cheeks burned with embarrassment. The whole paper had been far-fetched to begin with, and now it was even more ridiculous to think it was linked to Zartman's murder. Elizabeth suddenly wished she were an ostrich so she could bury her head in the sand and never have to face another living soul again.

The pounding headache increased, thundering like a hammer against her skull. The pulsating jazz music in the Coffee House would only make it worse. The quiet blandness of the cafeteria was exactly what Elizabeth needed right now.

Elizabeth dropped a quarter into the pay phone outside of the station and dialed Nina's number. "Hey, Nina, it's Liz again. Let's skip the Coffee House today. I'll meet you in the cafeteria, instead."

"I just got word from Nichols that she's going to be in the Coffee House in about twenty minutes." McKenna's voice intermingled with the static of the phone line. "Afterward, go to her dorm room and take everything that has to do with the paper. She lives in Dickenson Hall, room twenty-eight."

Pierce smoothed down his mustache with shaky fingertips. "How will I know it's her?"

"Do you see the bench next to you?"

Stepping away from the pay phone on the edge of campus, Pierce's eyes darted across the lawn. He spotted the nearest bench about five yards away. "Got it," he said into the receiver.

"You'll find a photo taped to the underside of the bench," McKenna instructed. "Bishop says this is the last job. As soon as it's over, you're free." Then the line went dead.

Pierce hung up the phone and strode over to the green wooden bench. Looking from side to side, he saw that no one was around, so he ran his hand on the underside of the bench until his fingers grazed the smooth paper envelope.

"Bingo," Pierce sighed aloud. He opened the envelope and pulled out the photograph inside. Elizabeth Wakefield's beautiful face smiled at him, looking so happy and trusting. A pang of guilt jabbed at his heart. Pierce quickly slipped the photo into his jacket pocket and headed for the Coffee House.

The pungent aroma of coffee wafted through the air as Pierce stepped inside the busy café. Small wooden tables covered with small white cups and flower vases cluttered the main floor of the Coffee House. Jazz music poured from stereo speakers bolted high on the brick walls. Pierce shoved his hands into his pockets and headed up the stairs to the second level. It was a balcony that overlooked the main floor—the perfect vantage point.

A waitress, with a tray of empty cups balanced on one shoulder, nudged Pierce's elbow. "Can I get you anything?"

"No, no. Not right now . . . maybe later," he stammered, shoving his hands deeper into his jacket pockets. The .45 magnum pressed hard against his hip.

The waitress looked him over. "Okay. Just give me a holler when you want something. You can sit wherever you want."

Pierce nodded, then bolted for the back table behind a large plastic palm tree. The table was pushed against the balcony railing, giving Pierce a clear view of the main floor below.

*There she is.* Pierce spotted Elizabeth immediately in the corner of the room. She was easily the most beautiful girl in the entire place. The sight of her golden blond hair and suntanned skin filled Pierce with pity. Elizabeth was so young and full of life. She had no idea what it was like to be in the real world and to have all your dreams shattered.

*How did you get mixed up in this?* Pierce asked Elizabeth silently. He took the gun out of his pocket and balanced it on his lap, under the table. Then he pulled out a cartridge filled with bullets and shoved the clip into the handle of the gun. *You won't feel a thing, I promise.*

Remorse and regret began chipping away at Pierce's sanity. The other three women didn't deserve to die, and neither did Elizabeth. But it was too late to change anything now. Elizabeth would be the last, and then he'd be free.

Pierce leaned closer to the balcony. *It's better this way, Elizabeth,* he thought silently as his finger curled around the trigger. *Everyone you know will betray you. I'm saving you a lot of heartache.* And with that, he raised his arm and aimed straight for her head.

"I can't believe you tried to pick up a guy in a cemetery," Lila Fowler said between dainty sips of café au lait. "That's a low for even *you.*"

"I wasn't trying to pick him up," Jessica shouted over the din of the Coffee House. "He just looked down-and-out. I wanted to help."

Isabella Ricci stirred her raspberry seltzer with a straw. "Come on, Li, you're being too hard on the girl. You know Jessica only helps available young men out of the goodness of her heart," she said with a wry smile. "Jessica Wakefield, Savior of the Distraught."

"I would've done the same thing if it had been a girl standing there." Jessica flipped her long blond hair over one shoulder. "I just wanted to help."

Lila and Isabella exchanged knowing glances before bursting out into hysterical laughter.

"What's so funny?" Jessica demanded.

"The hair flip is a dead giveaway." Isabella arched one perfectly shaped eyebrow. "He was cute, wasn't he?"

Strong, chiseled features and soft, golden eyes flashed through Jessica's mind. "Not really," she lied.

"So when are you guys going out?" Lila impatiently tapped her long red nails against the tabletop.

"We're not going anywhere together." Jessica took a sip of mocha. "I don't even know if he's still alive."

A look of horror came over Isabella's face. She tucked a strand of long black hair behind her ear. "What do you mean?"

Jessica smoothed down her miniskirt and crossed her legs. "As soon as I said, 'Don't kill yourself,' he took off."

*"Hey, baby, don't kill yourself."* Lila's ruby lips curled in mock disgust. "That has to be *the worst* pickup line of the decade!"

"You guys, this isn't a joke!" Jessica exclaimed, throwing her hands up in the air. "This guy could be dead for all we know, and it'd be my fault."

Isabella toyed with the patterned silk scarf tied around her slender throat. "You can't blame yourself for the irrational things this person might do."

"Maybe I should've followed him," Jessica said. "I could've talked some sense into him."

Lila shook her head. "You can't talk sense into people like that. Besides, there are thousands of

Julia Reynolds fans who are upset about her death. Are you going to go around helping every single one of them?"

"Of course not," Jessica answered. "But if I can help one person, then I should."

"Maybe Jess is right. If you have the opportunity to help someone, you should take it," Isabella said. She took a sip of seltzer. "And if you get a date out of it, then all the better!"

Lila folded her arms with determination. "Well, you two can waste your time with all the poor saps crying over Julia. *I'm* going straight for the top."

"Who's that?" Jessica asked.

Lila flashed her 100-megawatt smile. "Matt Barron. He's gorgeous, wealthy, famous, and oh-so-available. He's definitely going to need an understanding shoulder to cry on," she said with a wink.

"What about Bruce?" Isabella asked.

"I'm sure he'd understand," Lila said with a smirk. "Matt's a *star,* after all."

"Good luck finding Matt," Jessica said. "I've heard he went into hiding."

"I'll find him," Lila said confidently. "The Fowlers have connections."

Isabella shook her head. "Li, the poor guy just lost his fiancée. Now is not the time to be making moves on him."

"You're right." Lila's face fell. "I should wait until *next* week."

Jessica finished the last of the mocha and

pushed the empty cup away from her. "Is anyone up for—"

A loud, popping sound from overhead stopped Jessica mid-sentence. The music continued playing, and the students kept on talking, as though nothing had happened.

"What was that?" Lila asked as she craned her neck.

Isabella's brow furrowed. "Maybe it was the stereo."

"It sounded like—"

There was another pop, and the empty mocha cup in front of Jessica split apart into thousands of pieces. The bullet whizzed past and shattered the window behind her.

"Someone's got a gun!" Lila screamed.

Isabella grabbed Jessica's arm and yanked her under the small wooden table. The music stopped. Everyone started screaming at once, diving under tables and crawling toward the door. It was total chaos.

Jessica's heart pounded furiously in her ears as she took cover. "He almost hit me!"

"I can't believe this is happening," Isabella said shakily.

Lila moved slightly from under the table and looked around. Isabella grabbed her by the shoulder and pulled her back roughly. "Are you insane?" she screamed.

"I'm trying to see what's going on!" Lila shouted.

Jessica watched as dozens of feet and legs hurried past. "Maybe we should get out of here."

"The closest exit is to the right," Isabella pointed. "Let's make a run for it. On the count of the three—one . . . two . . ."

Jessica stuck her head out from under the table, and instantly another shot rang out. The three of them dove back under the table.

"When is it going to stop?" Jessica cried.

The shots kept coming, piercing the wall behind them. She closed her eyes, paralyzed with fear, wondering which shot was going to be the one to kill her.

"Take that!" Pierce shot three bullets into the old movie poster that hung on the back wall. He had been careful to hide himself in the cluster of artificial trees on the balcony. As far as he could tell, no one had seen him. When the trigger finally hit the dull click that signified an empty cartridge, he shoved the gun into his pocket and disappeared into the back stairwell.

"Let that be a warning to you, Elizabeth," Pierce said in the emptiness of the stairs. There would be hell to pay, of course, if Bishop ever found out he missed the shot, but Pierce couldn't help himself. He was hardly an expert at shooting firearms, and Elizabeth had been pretty far away from him. The first shot had been an honest effort, but as soon as he saw the look of absolute terror on Elizabeth's beautiful face, he knew he wouldn't be able to go through with it. So he shot around her, instead.

Pierce plowed through the back door, into the bright sunlight. He tucked the gun into the waistband of his jeans, then ripped off his windbreaker and tossed it into the green dumpster by the door. He also threw in his baseball cap and sunglasses. Wiping his sweaty face with the sleeve of his rugby shirt, Pierce coolly walked around the corner of the building to the quad.

"What a lovely day it is," he said aloud, looking up at the brilliant blue sky. Pierce walked casually down the path, feeling almost happy for the first time in nearly a week. The rampage in the Coffee House had been a good thing, he decided. Not only did it blow off a lot of tension to destroy everything in sight, but Pierce was proud of the fact that he had finally made a conscious decision not to hurt anyone else. He couldn't erase what he'd done to the other three women—the pain of causing their deaths was an enormous weight he'd have to bear for the rest of his life. But maybe, for once, he could turn things around and actually save someone, instead.

Pierce knocked on the door of Dickenson Hall's room twenty-eight and listened closely. No noise was coming from inside. In one smooth motion, he slipped into the room and closed the door behind him.

*Just grab the disks and mess things up a little,* Pierce calmly told himself. The important thing was to scare her. Maybe if Pierce was good enough at it, Bishop would decide to leave Elizabeth alone.

There were two desks in the room. One was covered with bottles of nail polish, hair curlers, and fashion magazines. The other had stacks of books and papers, and a computer.

"That's the one." Pierce walked over to the neater desk and rifled through the drawers. There were tons of computer disks, all carefully labeled and dated. At last, he found one marked "Julia Reynolds." Pierce tucked it away in his shirt pocket.

*There's probably a backup copy on the hard drive*, Pierce thought. He didn't have time to sit down and sort through Elizabeth's computer files; someone could walk in at any minute.

There was only one thing left to do.

"I'm sorry about this, Elizabeth," Pierce said aloud as he raised the computer high above his head, "but it's for your own good."

He heaved the computer against the wall, splintering pieces in all directions.

# Chapter Seven

"Elizabeth Wakefield is dead," Pierce announced as he tossed a computer disk on Bishop's desk. "I shot her."

Ronald Bishop smiled and took a cigar out of the wooden box on the corner of his desk. "Do you want one?" he offered.

"No, thanks," Pierce said with a nervous laugh. The tornado that had been raging inside him began winding down. It was the beginning of the end.

"Suit yourself." Bishop thrust the stogie in his mouth and walked over to the window, staring out over the horizon.

"I guess that means I'm free to go," Pierce said lightly. He had booked an afternoon flight for Missoula, Montana, his hometown. As soon as Bishop gave the word, Pierce was determined to leave Hollywood, never to return again.

"I said you're free to go when it's over," Bishop said calmly. "But it's not over. You didn't live up to your end of the bargain."

Pierce stiffened. "What do you mean?" he scoffed. "I killed four people for you, and Elizabeth Wakefield was the last one."

Bishop turned around suddenly, his fat lips curved into a sneer. "I can't believe you have the nerve to sit there and lie to me."

It was too late to turn back, so Pierce continued on. "I don't know what you're talking about," he said arrogantly.

"The Wakefield girl isn't dead, and you know it," Bishop spat out. "Or maybe you don't, because you took off before you had a chance to find out."

Pierce sat in silence, his fingers digging deep into the couch's leather upholstery.

Bishop took the cigar out of his mouth. His beady gray eyes bore down on Pierce like steel nails. "Do you think I'm stupid enough to make a deal with you and not check to see if you followed through?" He waved the cigar in the air to emphasize his point. "Right from the start I had the feeling you were going to bail out on me. So as a cautionary measure, I had someone follow you. I guess you proved that my instincts were right."

Something inside Pierce suddenly cracked and split wide open. Everything about him was exposed; nothing could be hidden from Bishop.

"I'm not cut out for this," he said anxiously.

"What? You're not a killer?" Bishop's eyes widened in feigned surprise. "For not being a killer, you've been pretty successful. With three deaths under your belt, you could call yourself a professional."

The tornado inside Pierce had regained its strength. Images of Julia and Kate, and of the frightened eyes of Elizabeth Wakefield swirled like a tempest inside his head. "I won't do it!" Pierce roared. "Find someone else."

"You want me to find someone else so you can squeal? You'd better think again," Bishop retorted. "You're going back to that campus, and you're going to finish her off."

Pierce's mustache twitched nervously. "I'm not doing your dirty work anymore."

Bishop towered over him, letting the burning ash of his cigar fall onto Pierce's lap. "Just keep one thing in mind, Killer—someone's always watching," Bishop threatened. "If you don't finish the job, you'll be next."

"I can't believe the police aren't doing anything about this," Nina said as she followed Elizabeth up the stairs to the second floor of Dickenson Hall. "Some maniac murders one of our professors, and the cops act like it's something that happens every day."

"Only the police chief acted that way," Elizabeth said, stopping at the top of the stairs.

"Detective Curtis took it seriously—that is, until he skipped off to Hawaii."

Nina's jaw dropped. "You mean they don't have anyone working the case?"

"Apparently not," Elizabeth said wearily. "There's nothing we can do."

As soon as they reached Elizabeth's room, the pounding in her head surged again with a blinding pressure. She reached for the doorknob to steady herself.

"Are you all right, Liz?" Nina asked, holding Elizabeth up.

"I'm fine," she answered breathlessly. "It's just a headache."

Nina's mouth was drawn back in a tight line. "Maybe you should forget about jogging this afternoon. You need to rest."

Elizabeth nodded. "Going to bed sounds like a great idea right now." Opening the door, she stepped inside.

Nina turned on the light. "Oh no!" she said, looking around the room.

Elizabeth clasped a hand over her mouth to stifle a scream. Her computer was a demolished heap in the middle of the room.

"Who would do this?" Nina's dark eyes bulged with horror.

Without answering, Elizabeth ran over to her desk and opened the top drawer. The disk containing "The Suicide Paper" was missing.

Panic penetrated every nerve in her body.

Someone had gotten very close, and Elizabeth sensed that they weren't too far away. "It's probably a rival journalist from another school," she said with forced lightness. The last thing she wanted was for Nina to know the truth. "You know, a college prank."

"Some prank," Nina said, picking up what was left of Elizabeth's computer keyboard. "You'd better call the police right away."

"No!" Elizabeth shrieked. She took a deep breath to gain her composure. "I mean, they won't do anything about it."

Nina reached for the phone. "Liz, don't be silly. You have to report it."

Elizabeth grabbed her aching forehead. It felt as if a bulldozer were plowing its way through her skull. "Do me a favor—call Tom, instead."

Elizabeth reached into her closet and grabbed a black duffel bag.

"Tom, this is Nina. I'm calling for Liz. Hold on a sec, I'll put her on." Nina held the receiver out in midair. "He's on the phone."

Elizabeth shook her head. She grabbed a pair of jeans and a sweatshirt and shoved them into the bag. "Don't tell him what happened, just say that something's come up, and I need his help."

Nina looked bewildered. "Liz, what's going on?"

"Just do it."

After a moment, Nina put the phone against her ear again. "Liz wants me to tell you that something's come up, and she needs your help." She listened for a moment, then spoke to Elizabeth. "What do you want him to do?"

A hairbrush, toothbrush, and soap were all thrown into the bag. "Tell him to meet me at the boardwalk tonight with as much cash as he can spare."

Nina relayed the message. There was a pause. "He wants to know what happened."

Elizabeth packed a flashlight and an extra pair of sneakers. "I'll explain later."

"She'll explain later," Nina said into the phone. "I'm just as confused by all this as you are, Tom." She hung up the receiver. "What's gotten into you?" Nina demanded.

Elizabeth zipped up her bag. "I wish I could tell you, but I can't. I'm not quite sure what's going on myself." She tied her hair back into a ponytail and grabbed the keys to the Jeep. "I've got to hide out for a while. If anyone asks where I am, say that there was a family emergency, and I went home."

"Liz, you're scaring me," Nina cried. "If you did something wrong, I'll understand. But *please* tell me what's happening."

Elizabeth gave Nina a hug. "I didn't do anything, but suddenly things have become very complicated." Her blue-green eyes were damp with tears. "If anything happens, I want you to know that you've been a great friend, and I love you."

A tear rolled down Nina's cheek. "Take care of yourself," she sobbed. "I'll see you when you get back."

"I'm here to see Kate Morgan." Matt Barron smiled politely at the receptionist. He had managed to make himself presentable for the meeting by taking a shower and throwing on some of the clothes Bridget had brought back from the cleaners. "I have a one o'clock appointment."

The woman behind the desk at the *Hollywood Daily* turned pale. Suddenly the phone rang, and she snatched it off the hook. "I'll be with you in a moment, Mr. Barron," she said quickly.

Matt nodded and took a seat in the gray and burgundy waiting room. The receptionist's strange demeanor didn't faze him at all. Ever since Julia had died, everyone he came in contact with acted peculiar. Many of them, especially his close friends, probably didn't know what to do or say under such tragic circumstances. The other people, who didn't know him so well, may have thought of him as some sort of oddity—a freak. After all, it could only take a monster to drive a beautiful, talented, and successful woman to kill herself.

*But that's all going to change,* Matt thought to himself. He watched the somber faces of newspaper reporters as they silently marched around the office, carrying cardboard boxes. *As soon as Kate Morgan tells me what she knows, I'll be on my way to finding out who murdered Julia.* Matt's throat tightened with bittersweet relief. He hoped that Kate really had a piece of significant information, that she wasn't leading him on just to get an exclusive interview.

The receptionist hung up the phone. "Mr. Barron, could I speak with you for a moment?"

Matt approached the sleek, modern-looking desk. "Will Ms. Morgan be ready soon?" he asked hopefully.

The receptionist looked at him gravely. "I'm afraid she won't meeting with you—"

"We can always reschedule. I can meet her whenever she wants."

"That won't be necessary, Mr. Barron. I'm sorry to tell you this, but something terrible has happened," she said in a hushed voice. "Yesterday, Kate Morgan was murdered."

Matt fell against the desk. "What?"

"The police have no suspect and no motive," the receptionist said. "We're all very distressed about this."

Matt ran a hand through his freshly washed hair. *What am I going to do now?* In the tumultuous ocean of speculation, Kate Morgan was like a beacon, leading Matt to solid ground. Now that she was dead, his chances of finding Julia's murderer were slipping through his fingers like grains of sand.

"Is there anyone I could speak with?" His golden eyes pleaded with her. "It's very important."

"Of course." The receptionist sighed heavily. "Kate's office is around the corner. Someone should be able to help you."

Matt headed for the office. A line of people filed out of the office, each carrying a box. Their faces showed various states of shock and grief.

"Excuse me," Matt said to a balding man who stood by the door. "I was wondering if you could help me."

The man's face was gaunt. He picked up a box of books and handed it to a co-worker. "Sure, what is it?"

Matt extended his hand. "I'm Matt Barron. First, let me say that I'm terribly sorry about what happened to Kate."

"I'm David Wyse." The man shook Matt's hand. "It's such a waste. Kate was a wonderful person. These lunatics that roam the streets commit horrible crimes without ever stopping to think about all the people they're affecting. No value for human life." He shook his head tearfully. "I understand you've had a tragedy in your own life recently. I'm very sorry."

"Thank you. The past week has been an absolute nightmare." Matt exhaled loudly. "And that's why I'm here. I was supposed to meet with Kate. She said she had some information about Julia that I would want to know."

David pulled a stack of books off the shelf and packed them in a box. "She didn't mention anything about it to me. It was probably personal."

Matt stepped aside to make room for more people in the office. They started taking Kate's diplomas and awards down from the wall. "Do you think she would tell anyone else?"

"Knowing Kate, probably not," David said. "But maybe there's something here in her office." He looked around for a moment. "I know it must seem odd that we're packing up her things so quickly, but it was just too painful to let it sit here. Every time one of us would go by, we'd practically have a nervous breakdown. We kept expecting her to come back."

*I know the feeling.* Matt recalled the empty marble hallway of Julia's apartment and how he longed to hear her voice echoing from room to room. "Would you mind if I took a quick look on her desk?"

"Be my guest," David said. "But we've already packed up most of it."

Matt slowly walked over to the desk. The drawers were empty, and all that remained was sitting on the desktop. He moved the papers slightly, as if he were afraid to disturb anything. Carefully, he worked his way through newspaper clippings, typed stories, and notebook papers littered with doodled drawings.

At last, his eyes rested on a pink piece of paper from a message pad. Julia's name was scrawled on it, along with the words "Elizabeth Wakefield at SVU" and a phone number Matt didn't recognize.

"Did you find anything?" David asked.

Matt tucked the piece of paper into his black leather jacket. "I hope so," he answered.

"Oh, Liz! You're not going to believe what happened." The color had drained from Jessica's face, and she looked visibly shaken.

"I know all about it," Elizabeth said tiredly. She carried the black duffel bag with one hand and grabbed Jessica's elbow with the other, steering her toward the student parking lot.

"How did you find out?" Jessica's voice shook as she spoke. "Who told you?"

"No one." Elizabeth's eyes scanned the quad for faces she didn't recognize. "Nina and I went back to the room, and we saw it."

Jessica's brow wrinkled in confusion. "Saw what?"

"My computer smashed to pieces on the floor. Do you have any idea when it happened?"

Jessica stopped dead in her tracks. "Liz, I didn't know anything about your computer. I was talking about what happened at the Coffee House."

The hairs on the back of Elizabeth's neck stood straight up. "What happened at the Coffee House?"

Jessica threw her arms around her sister's neck. "It was awful." Tears sprung instantly to her eyes. "I was having coffee with Lila and Izzy when someone started shooting at us. I don't know who it was . . . but they just kept shooting!"

A shriek of fright rose to Elizabeth's throat, but she used all of her strength to keep it down. "Was anyone hurt?"

"No. We crawled under the table for cover," Jessica whimpered. "The weird thing was that it was like they were shooting directly at me, no one else." Jessica leaned her head on her twin's shoulder. "Liz, I've never been so terrified in my whole life."

A numbing realization took hold of Elizabeth, chilling her to the bone. *They thought it was me in the Coffee House,* she realized with shock. *They wanted to kill me.* But who could've known she was going to be there?

Jessica wiped her eyes. "And now your computer's wrecked. The whole thing is so creepy," she said. "Did you call the police?"

*The police.* Images of Chief Nichols flashed through Elizabeth's mind. He'd been so condescending to her earlier in the day. He wasn't even willing to at least check out her theory. Hot anger boiled inside Elizabeth. If anything happened to her or Jessica, he'd be responsible.

"You've got to call the police," Jessica said.

*Call the police.* Suddenly, like the sun breaking through storm clouds, everything became clear to Elizabeth. Chief Nichols had heard her phone call to Nina. He was the only one who'd known she was going to be at the Coffee House.

"Oh no," Elizabeth said slowly. "He was in on it the whole time."

"*Who* was in on *what*?" Jessica asked.

Elizabeth's pulse quickened. She grabbed Jessica's arm, dragging her toward the parking lot. "There isn't time now—I'll tell you on the way." Her pace increased with each step.

"Where are we going?" Jessica demanded, stumbling to keep up with her sister.

Elizabeth's heart leaped into her throat. "We're going underground."

# Chapter Eight

Tom heard the back door of his car open. He cut the engine and turned his head around. "Great timing, Liz. I just got—"

"Turn around and do as you're told," the voice commanded.

Tom turned back around and faced the boardwalk. Night was beginning to fall, and young couples were walking along the beach, taking in the romantic view.

A rustling sound came from the backseat. Tom felt the jabbing of elbows and knees against his back. "Need more room back there?" he said with amusement as he pulled the seat forward.

"She said *'don't move'*!" a second voice sneered.

Tom recognized the voice immediately. *"Jess?* What are you doing here?"

"Tom, please, don't talk," Elizabeth whispered.

"Just stare straight ahead. It's important to make it look like you're here alone."

"I know what's going on," Tom laughed as he spoke through tight lips. "You want to elope, but your parents found out, and your dad is coming after me with a shotgun."

Elizabeth's voice softened. "Tom, this is really serious. Please stop making jokes."

It was the pleading tone in Elizabeth's voice that made him realize that she wasn't kidding. "I'm sorry," he whispered. "There's a blanket on the shelf near the rear window if you want to cover up."

There was a bit more shuffling as the two girls settled in. A strange, prickling sensation gnawed at the base of Tom's spine. Elizabeth had been in weird circumstances before, but something told him that this time it could be really big. Maybe even dangerous.

"Did you bring the money?" Elizabeth asked.

"I took out five hundred dollars," Tom said. "Almost everything in my account—it would've been a lousy honeymoon."

A police car pulled alongside Tom's Saturn. A burly officer stepped out of the vehicle and approached the driver's side.

Tom swallowed hard and continued to look straight ahead. "Sit tight, ladies. We have a visitor." There was much commotion as Elizabeth and Jessica hunkered down to the floor of the car.

The officer knocked on the window.

Tom turned suddenly, as if surprised, and rolled down the window. "Good evening, officer," he said with a bright smile. "What can I do for you?"

The officer stared hard at Tom. One eye was wide open, while the other squinted, as if he were practicing how to wink. "What are you doing out here?"

"Just admiring the beautiful view, sir." Tom pointed to the beach. "I'm a surfer, and I thought I'd check to see how the waves are tonight."

The officer's face crinkled suspiciously. "It's low tide. A surfer would know that."

Tom nodded vigorously in agreement. "An *expert* surfer would know that. As you can tell, I'm just a beginner," Tom sputtered. "It sounds like you know a lot about surfing, yourself, Officer. Do you hit the waves much?"

The officer straightened up a bit, his thick middle pressing against the car door. "Do you realize that you're parked in a restricted zone?"

Tom's eyes rested on the traffic sign a few feet away. It read No Parking from 7 P.M. to 7 A.M.

"By law, I have the right to tow you," the officer said humorlessly. "May I see your license and registration?"

As Tom took out his license and reached for the glove compartment, the officer turned on his flashlight and directed the beam inside the car.

"Here it is!" Tom shoved the license and registration at the officer. A thin film of sweat covered his forehead. What would he do if they towed his car? Tom imagined trying to explain to the officer why he was hiding two girls in the backseat.

The officer took the license from him, looking more than slightly annoyed. He peered intensely at Tom and compared him to the picture on the license. "I should tow you."

"I know. And I would understand if you did. You're just doing your job." Tom felt a sharp jab in his kidneys from Elizabeth. "But I want you to know that I'm terribly sorry, and I had no intention of hurting anyone."

The officer sighed. "All right, then," he said gruffly. "But you've got two minutes to move it outta here."

"No problem," Tom said with a cheerful tone. "It doesn't look like the surfing's going to be good tonight, anyway."

The officer gave Tom a look of disgust, then moved away from the car.

Tom rolled up the window. "Okay, he's gone. You can breathe easy." He started the engine. "I hope you didn't want to hang around here—we've got to get moving."

"That's okay," Elizabeth said from under the blanket. "It's better if we don't stay in one spot too long."

The prickly feeling returned at the base of Tom's spine. "Now can you tell me what's going on?"

"Not yet," Elizabeth said. "First you need to

bring us to the closest drugstore. Then I'll need fifty dollars for a rental car. We'll split up, then you'll meet us at the Birchwood Motel in Middleton."

Tom pulled out of the parking spot and onto the main road. "Is this some kind of elaborate joke?"

Elizabeth reached out from under the blanket and rested her hand on his. "I only wish."

"I hate to leave you like this," Bridget said as she stood up and smoothed the creases out of her cream-colored business suit. "But I think this trip to New York is crucial if we want to nip any negative publicity in the bud."

Matt sat back on his black leather couch and watched the bright fish in the coffee-table aquarium swimming in erratic circles. "First my love life is destroyed, and now my career is going down the tubes," he said with a rueful smile. "I love this business."

"Your career is *not* going down the tubes. It just needs a little reworking." Bridget picked up a few pieces of plastic-wrapped dry cleaning that were laying on the couch and hung them in the hall closet. "There are a few reporters on the East Coast who are trying to play up your involvement in Julia's death. The key words here are *damage control*," she called from the hallway. "Maybe with a little gentle persuasion, I can get them to turn their stories around."

Matt leaned his head against the back of the couch. "I know a surefire way to shut those reporters up. As soon as I find the people responsible for Julia's murder, they'll turn around."

Bridget's high heels clicked against the black-and-white tile floor as she walked back to the living room. She stopped directly in front of Matt, her arms folded boldly in front of her. "Don't do that to yourself, Matt. It's self-destructive."

"What are you talking about?" Matt's golden eyes widened. "What's so destructive about finding my fiancée's murderer?"

Bridget sighed. "First of all, we don't have any proof that she was murdered. At best it was probably an accident," she said matter-of-factly. "The point is, I'd hate to see you wrap yourself up in this crazy idea of yours, which has no basis in reality."

"I'm not the only person who didn't believe it was a suicide. Kate Morgan knew there was more to the story," he said defensively. "I don't know what it was that she had to tell me, but I'm going to find out."

Taking a seat beside him, Bridget placed a sympathetic hand on Matt's arm. "You've been under an enormous amount of stress lately, but you can't run around chasing these wild ideas of yours. Especially since you have absolutely no proof. Julia wouldn't want you to do it," Bridget said carefully. "Matt, you need to let it go."

Matt's jaw tensed. *I'll never let it go*, he

114

thought with staunch determination, *as long as Julia's murderer runs free.* As much as he respected Bridget's opinion, it didn't matter to Matt that she didn't understand what he was going through. It didn't matter if anyone did. Deep in his gut, Matt knew that Kate Morgan died because of something she knew. Someone was trying to keep her quiet. And Matt wouldn't rest until he found out who it was.

Bridget gave Matt a dry kiss on the cheek and handed him a business card with a handwritten phone number on it. "That's where I'll be staying in New York. Call me if you need *anything,*" she said as she got up from the couch. "Everything will go smoothly, so don't fret. I'll see you in a couple of weeks."

Matt squeezed her hand. "Have a safe trip, and thanks again."

Bridget waved at him and showed herself out. The very same moment that Matt heard the front door close, the phone rang.

Matt ignored the ring, then suddenly a thought dawned on him. *What if it's David Wyse at the* Hollywood Daily? *Maybe he's found out something about Julia.* . . . Matt lunged hopefully toward the phone.

"Hello?"

There was a pause, then a squeaky voice said, "Is this Matt Barron?"

"Yeah, who's this?"

"You can call me Gomez," the voice suddenly

dropped down an octave. It was obvious that the person at the other end was trying to disguise his voice. "I have some information about Julia's death."

Matt's heart stopped. "What do you know?" he choked into the receiver.

"It's more complicated than it seems," the voice said huskily. "You should definitely investigate."

"Where do I start?" Matt stretched the telephone cord as far as it would go to snatch a paper and pen off of a black-lacquered writing table in the corner of the room. "Give me something to go on."

"That's all I can say right now. You need to check things out." There was a nervous edge to Gomez's voice.

Matt's mouth suddenly went dry. "At least give me your phone number so I can get in touch with you."

Suddenly, the line went dead.

Matt dropped the receiver and covered his face with his hands. Once again, he'd been so incredibly close to finding something out, only to have it ripped away from him at the last minute. The secret to Julia's death loomed ahead of him like a mirage in the desert, taunting and teasing him until he was about to go mad. If only one good thing came out of the experience, it was the confirmation of his instincts. Julia's death was no accident—she was murdered.

*Don't lose hope yet,* a voice inside his head told him. *You still have one more clue to go on.* Matt pulled out the pink slip of paper he had found on Kate Morgan's desk. His fingers traced the letters on the paper, scrawled in blue ink. It was the phone number of a college student named Elizabeth Wakefield. *What could she possibly know about Julia's death?* he wondered.

Matt picked up the receiver and dialed the number. The phone rang. "Come on, Elizabeth. You're my last hope," he whispered under his breath. Matt closed his eyes as he listened to the ringing over and over again, praying someone would answer the phone.

Tom stared at Elizabeth in disbelief. "Are you *sure* the police chief was the only person who knew you were going to the Coffee House?"

Elizabeth unwrapped a tiny bar of soap with Birchwood Motel printed on it and washed her face at the sink. "Stop acting like I've made all this up in my head," she said, drying her face with a thin white towel. "I'm the most rational person in the world—and this is the best explanation I can come up with."

Jessica turned the television dial from one snowy station to another. "This stupid thing doesn't even come with a remote control!" She whacked the side of the console with her hand, and the picture cleared for a split second before disintegrating into black-and-white static.

"Look, I'm sorry," Tom said to Elizabeth as he sat down on the sagging double bed. "It's just a lot for me to take in all at once. It's hard to believe that a paper you wrote could get you into so much trouble."

Elizabeth pulled the plastic cover off a drinking glass and filled it with a few grayish-looking ice cubes. "I can hardly believe it, either," she said. "In fact, the whole idea that a movie studio would plot to kill a famous actress seemed completely ridiculous to me. But obviously, I was close to the mark. Close enough for the people involved to get scared."

"I guess anything's possible," Tom said, sprawling out over the burnt-orange-and-brown-striped bedcover. "For example, until today, I never would've believed that a maniac could walk into the Coffee House and start using the student body as target practice."

Jessica clicked off the TV. "What happened with that? Did they find a suspect?"

Tom shook his head. "Dean Schreeve tried to play down the whole thing, to keep the students calm. He chalked it up to some fraternity prank."

"Fraternity prank!" Jessica shrilled. "I was almost killed today, and they're acting like it was some sort of joke?"

"That's just the way school politics work," Elizabeth said, sitting on the bed next to Tom. "I'm sure they're checking things out, but in the meantime, they have to quell everyone's fears. If students started leaving SVU in droves, the school would be in serious financial trouble."

"Not to mention all the bad press SVU would get," Tom added.

Jessica strolled over to the wood-veneer dresser and peeked into the bag Elizabeth had brought from the drugstore. "I hope they find that psycho soon." Jessica pouted. "Until then, my social life is on hold!"

Tom threw a flat pillow at Jessica. "Oh, what a tragedy!"

"Laugh all you want," Jessica whined. "But I was supposed to go out with the new Swedish exchange student, Niklas Eriksson, tonight. We were going to go gliding in his ultralight plane!"

"Chill out, Jess!" Elizabeth rolled her eyes. "Until this thing blows over, we have to hang loose." She picked up a box of hair dye and started reading the instructions on the back. *I don't know what's worse,* she thought miserably to herself. *Being stalked by a madman, or being imprisoned with my twin.*

"What's this?" Jessica shrieked, yanking the box out of her sister's hand. "Don't get any bright ideas," she said, looking at the picture on the front. "There's no way I'm dyeing my hair pumpkin orange. Why couldn't you have picked a nice auburn, instead?"

Elizabeth snatched the box back. "I just grabbed the first box on the shelf," she said coldly.

"Excuse me for not being fashion-conscious when I'm fearing for my life!"

"Okay, you two, let's all stay cool," Tom intervened. "You're not going to be much help to each other if you fight the whole time." He turned to Elizabeth. "So what should I do now?"

Elizabeth held his hand tightly. "I need you to get some things out of my room."

"I don't feel right about leaving you."

"We'll be okay," she promised, giving his hand a squeeze. "But I really need those articles about New Vision and Mammoth that I left on my desk. And I also need my address book."

Tom stared deeply into Elizabeth's sad eyes. "Are you sure you're going to be okay?"

Jessica yawned loudly. "Yeah, yeah, she'll be fine," she said dryly.

Elizabeth leaned closer and kissed Tom's warm, soft lips. "I'm going to miss you," she said.

"Me too." He breathed into her golden hair. "But I'll be back first thing tomorrow. Take care of yourself, and don't open the door for anyone."

"I won't." Elizabeth threw her arms around him. The strength and security of his embrace made her feel as if she were floating high above the clouds, free from fear and danger.

Tom let go, and instantly Elizabeth felt as though she were crashing back to earth.

"Stay safe," he said, cupping Elizabeth's face in his hands and kissing her one last time. "I'll see you tomorrow."

Elizabeth's eyes were moist with tears. "Bye."

"Is the soap opera finished?" Jessica said as soon as Tom left.

"Yes." Elizabeth sniffled.

"Good, because I'm starved," Jessica said, patting her stomach. "Where are we going to eat?"

Elizabeth sighed. "I don't think it's such a good idea to leave the room. What if someone sees us?"

"Don't worry, we'll be fine," Jessica said as she threw on her jean jacket. "They'd never think to look for us in this dinky little town."

A gum-snapping waitress in thick-soled shoes directed Jessica and Elizabeth to a booth in the back of the diner. She handed them two laminated menus. "The special tonight is chicken potpie," she said mechanically as she wiped ketchup stains off the green marbleized tabletop. "Can I get you ladies anything to drink?"

"I'll have a root beer, no ice," Jessica said, opening her menu.

Elizabeth traced her finger over the silver-colored duct tape that covered the rip in the leatherette seat. "Just water for me, thanks."

"Be back in a jiffy," the waitress said in a flat tone. She turned and headed for the kitchen, her shoes squeaking across the grimy floor as she walked.

Jessica peered at the menu. "Mmm, I just love motel restaurants," she said bitingly. "Will it be

121

the liver and onion platter or the baked tuna surprise? I can't decide."

"Be happy you're eating at all," Elizabeth scolded. "It's not safe to leave the motel. Someone might spot us."

Jessica toyed with the napkin dispenser. "I hope you're right about this whole conspiracy thing, because if I have to spend three days in this hick town for nothing, heads are gonna roll."

Elizabeth's lips pinched angrily. "Save it, Jess. I think you have a crazy notion that I actually *like* this. Believe me, I don't like it any more than you do."

The motel restaurant was fairly quiet at such a late hour, but Elizabeth had the sneaking suspicion that this was probably as busy as it ever got. A couple in their sixties was sitting at a booth by the front windows, sharing a piece of pie. A young man with a mustache, who looked like he was in his early twenties, sat at the counter, sipping coffee. Only one cook was operating the grill, singing tunelessly to an old song on the radio.

"Made up your mind yet?" the waitress said, setting two paper cups down on the table. She shoved the cup of root beer at Elizabeth, then pulled it back again. "You both look exactly alike—I can't remember who ordered what."

"The root beer's mine," Jessica said, taking the cup.

Elizabeth took the water. "I'll have the special—the chicken pie."

The waitress snapped her gum loudly. "Coleslaw, french fries?"

"Coleslaw, please," Elizabeth said politely. Her gaze traveled from the menu to the lunch counter, where she caught the young man staring at them.

Jessica handed her menu to the waitress. "I want a cheeseburger with sliced avocado and sprouts. And a side order of fried zucchini."

The waitress laughed. It was a high, squeaky laugh, much like the sound of her shoes when she walked. "Look, miss, the only thing green I have to put on burgers is a slice of pickle. Is that all right with you?"

"I guess so," Jessica sighed.

"And we don't fry zucchini here. We only fry potatoes."

Jessica rolled her eyes to the ceiling. "Whatever."

The waitress squeaked off to the kitchen, and Elizabeth leaned across the table. "You didn't have to be so rude," she whispered to Jessica.

"I just wanted to see if they had anything else, that's all," Jessica answered. "Maybe they never even thought of frying zucchini before."

Elizabeth looked back at the counter, where the young man was sitting. He was still staring in their direction. His face was pasty white, and his eyes were weary. He gazed at them intently, as though he were watching. And waiting.

"Don't turn around," Elizabeth commanded.

123

She took a sip of water. "There's a guy at the counter who's staring at us."

Jessica tossed her hair over one shoulder. "Is he cute?"

The back of Elizabeth's neck tingled. "It doesn't matter. He's giving me the creeps."

"Everybody gives you the creeps these days," Jessica said with disgust. "Did it ever occur to you that we're the best-looking women in this whole restaurant? That's why he's staring."

"It's more than that." Elizabeth stole a few glances in his direction. "He's studying us."

The young man's eyes were glazed, and his stare was unswerving. Elizabeth wasn't exactly sure if he was one of the people who wanted them dead, but she wasn't about to stick around to find out.

"I hope the food's good," Jessica said. "I feel like I haven't eaten in days."

The waitress came out of the kitchen, holding a steaming pot of coffee. She stood directly in front of the young man as she filled his cup, blocking his view of Jessica and Elizabeth's booth.

Elizabeth's stomach worked itself into a tight knot. *This is your only chance,* a voice whispered in her ear. *Take it now.*

Instantly, Elizabeth was on her feet, dragging her twin toward the ladies' bathroom.

"Hey, what's going on?" Jessica whined. The elderly couple by the window turned to stare at them. "What about our food?" she asked.

Elizabeth threw Jessica into the tiny bathroom and locked the door. "Can't you keep quiet? You almost blew it for us!"

Jessica stuck out her lower lip. "I'm hungry! What are we doing in here?"

Elizabeth leaned her back against the wall near the paper-towel dispenser. "I think that guy was after us," she said shakily. "It might've been our only chance to get away."

"You were afraid of that harmless guy?" Jessica asked incredulously. "Talk about paranoid. Face it, Liz. You're totally losing it."

"I don't want any more coffee," Pierce said impatiently to the waitress. She stood directly in front of him, completely blocking his view of Elizabeth Wakefield and her twin sister.

The waitress smiled flirtatiously. "Oh, come on. You look like you need a little pick-me-up."

Pierce strained to look around her without being obvious. Every nerve in his body throbbed from anxiety and too much caffeine. He placed his hand over the top of the coffee mug. "No, really. I've had enough."

"What are you in such a hurry for?" The waitress peeled his fingers off the rim of the cup. "Stay a while and enjoy the coffee," she said, filling the cup all the way to the top.

*Don't say a word and maybe she'll go away,* Pierce thought silently. He leaned to the side a bit to see how things were going in Elizabeth's booth.

"I'll be around," the waitress said with a wink. "Just shout if you need me."

Pierce forced a smile, grateful that she was finally going to leave him alone. The waitress stepped aside, and that's when he saw that the booth was empty.

*Where did they go?* Pierce thought in panic. He was sitting by the door, so if they'd left he definitely would've seen them. Every space in the restaurant was wide open; there was no place they could be hiding. *Except the bathroom.*

Pierce took a jolting sip of hot coffee. He couldn't believe Elizabeth had a twin sister. Elizabeth was a smart girl—he could tell just by looking at her. It had taken her no time at all to figure out that Bishop's people were on to her. She was on the run right away. If Bishop had believed Pierce, she probably would've escaped without any trouble. But now he was on her heels, and he wouldn't rest until she was dead.

"You should see this gorgeous coconut cream pie I made this afternoon," the waitress shouted from the kitchen. She held the pie proudly in the air. "Do you want a slice? You can be the first to taste it!"

"No, thanks," Pierce said blandly. His eyes were riveted to the bathroom door. Elizabeth and her sister had been in there almost five minutes by now. Long enough to escape. Part of him hoped they'd made it.

Bishop's voice suddenly echoed in Pierce's

head. *"If you don't finish the job, you'll be next."* A sudden chill shook the very core of him, working its way deep into Pierce's bones. Slowly, he swiveled the stool around to face the front windows. Parked in the space in front of the building was a sleek black Cadillac. In the driver's seat was a man Pierce didn't recognize, but his stony glare told Pierce all he needed to know.

*"Someone's always watching."*

Pierce poured the coffee down his throat, the hot liquid burning the entire way down. He slapped two dollars down on the counter and strode over to the bathroom door. There was nothing more he could do. He had no choice but to kill them both.

# Chapter Nine

"He's standing outside the door!" Jessica warned as she peeked through the keyhole. The young man walked around in a circle, as if he were growing impatient waiting for them. Once again, Elizabeth's instincts had been right.

"What's he doing now?" Elizabeth whispered. Her voice was strong and steady, but edged with fear.

Jessica looked at Elizabeth, her eyes as big as silver dollars. "I don't think he's going to wait much longer."

The man outside the door walked toward them and fiddled with the doorknob. Jessica backed away quickly, her stomach doing a complete somersault.

Elizabeth pulled her sister close and whispered in her ear. "There's only one way out of here," she said. Then she pointed to the narrow window near the ceiling.

Jessica nodded weakly. What else could they do? Then there was a knock at the door.

Gripped with fear, Jessica froze. Elizabeth impulsively flushed the toilet. "I'll be out in a minute," she called, before moving over to the sink and turning the water on full blast.

"I'll hoist you up," Elizabeth directed. "Then when you're outside, reach in and pull me out."

Elizabeth laced her fingers, making a step for Jessica. Jessica stepped into it, like she'd done a thousand times during Sweet Valley High football games. *Good thing I was a cheerleader,* she thought gratefully, as Elizabeth pushed her into the air.

Jessica hooked the edge of her foot on one of the exposed water pipes and reached for the windowsill. When her footing was steady, she secured the other foot on the paper-towel dispenser. She stuck her torso out the narrow window, and with a final push from Elizabeth, Jessica made it out the window.

There was a second knock at the door, this one more urgent than the first.

"Hurry!" Jessica called down to her twin. Her feet balanced precariously on the outside ledge, and her arms dangled through the window. "Give me your hand!"

Elizabeth stepped into the sink and held on to the water pipes. With one foot, she stretched to reach the paper-towel dispenser. Elizabeth caught it with her toe, but couldn't pull herself up any higher.

Jessica moved herself closer to the window, stretching as far down as she possibly could. "Can you reach?"

Elizabeth's mouth was tense. She teetered for a moment, clutching the water pipes.

"Grab my hand!"

Elizabeth let go of the pipes, one hand at a time, firmly grabbing Jessica's wrists. Jessica pulled with all her strength, but Elizabeth didn't budge. Backing up a little farther, Jessica heaved again. This time, Elizabeth was able to get a better foothold on the towel dispenser and pushed herself up to the window.

"We made it!" Jessica cheered, jumping to the pavement below. Elizabeth followed.

Jessica looked around at the deserted back lot of the motel restaurant. It was a quiet, moonless night. Even the trees were eerily still. It was like the heavy, airless silence that descends before a storm erupts.

"We can't go back to the motel room, they know we're staying here," Elizabeth said, her brow creased with worry. "We need to go someplace where we can get lost. Someplace big."

Jessica looked up into the black sky. "I guess there's only one place to go," she said into the dead air. "We'd better head for L.A."

"Could you please give me Elizabeth Wakefield's room number?" Matt asked the student behind the information desk. Through his dark sunglasses, he could see that the student union was alive with activity, bustling with students on their way to early morning classes. They congregated in packs near the mailboxes and in front of the bookstore, their faces energetic and alive.

The student at the desk opened a thick book and ran his finger down the page, stopping an inch from the bottom. "Dickenson Hall, room twenty-eight," he said.

Matt made a note on the same pink paper he'd found on Kate Morgan's desk. "And how do I get to Dickenson Hall?"

The student pointed straight ahead toward the glass doors at the main entrance. "Follow the path past the library, then take a right. It's the second dorm on your left."

"Thanks," Matt said. Shoving the paper into his pocket, he hurried out the door, into the bright morning sunlight.

Matt walked rapidly down the path toward Dickenson Hall. He had let his beard grow in full, hoping it would be enough of a disguise. But as a precaution, Matt was careful not to look in anyone's direction, just in case they might recognize him. Bridget was a great publicist, and there was no doubt that nearly every student at SVU knew who Matt Barron was or had at least heard of him. Even with all the benefits that came with being famous, Matt still missed the solitude he'd had when no one knew him. Being able to go out in public without being recognized and never having cameras shoved in your face seemed like paradise to him now.

Matt opened the door to Dickenson Hall and walked into the lobby. A young woman in running gear was standing by the soda machine. Matt stopped in his tracks, waiting for the familiar light of recognition to flash in her eyes before she asked, *"Could I have your autograph? I've seen all your movies."*

But her eyes didn't light up. In fact, she looked a little pale and shaken.

Matt scratched his dark beard and smiled charmingly at the woman. "Excuse me, miss. Could you tell me how to get to room twenty-eight? I'm here to see Elizabeth Wakefield."

"If you don't mind me asking, who are you, and why are you here?" the woman asked, her voice tinged with suspicion.

Matt smiled to himself, deeply pleased that she didn't recognize him. "I'm Elizabeth's cousin," Matt said with confidence. "She's not expecting me—we haven't seen each other in years. But I was in the area, so I thought I'd drop by and say hello."

"Too bad you weren't here yesterday," the woman said, cracking open a can of soda, "I saw her leave last night in a hurry, with a bag packed. She told everybody that there was a family emergency and she had to get home. But I think there was another reason."

Matt's heart sank in his chest. He had to

find her. "Why do you think she left?"

The woman took a long drink from her can of soda, then set it down on the floor by her feet. "This campus has been completely insane lately." Her face became paler as she spoke. "A journalism professor was killed by a mail bomb, then some psycho started shooting in the middle of the Coffee House. It's getting so that I'm scared to even leave my dorm," she said intensely. "To be honest, I don't blame Liz for taking off. I'm ready to leave this place, too."

*Now what am I supposed to do?* Matt combed his hands through his hair impatiently. The search for the truth about Julia seemed to get longer and longer all the time, and there were always obstacles getting in his way. Matt felt like a laboratory rat in one of those test mazes: With every turn he made, he ended up hitting a wall.

"She lives right at the top of the stairs," the young woman said. "If you want, you could leave her a note under her door."

"I think I will. Thanks," Matt said. *Maybe Elizabeth left some clue as to where she went,* he thought as he ran up the stairs, taking them two at a time..He'd scour the entire room until he found something.

Matt slid a credit card in the crack of the door and jimmied it open. He stepped inside and saw the smashed computer on the floor. Someone was obviously hot on Elizabeth's trail. He hoped whoever it was hadn't reached her yet.

On the top of the desk closest to the door was a red leather address book. Matt flipped through the pages. Kate Morgan was listed, and underneath was the name of a Professor Zartman. *I wonder if she's the same professor who was killed?* The more he thought about it, the more it made sense that the strange events that had been happening on campus were related. Elizabeth had some important information, and someone desperately wanted to keep her from talking.

Suddenly, Matt heard someone jiggling the door handle. He put the address book in his jacket pocket and dove into the closet. *Please let it be Elizabeth.*

The door opened, and someone stepped inside. Matt cracked the closet door and peered out. It was a young guy with sandy brown hair, wearing khaki shorts and a dark green T-shirt. He walked right over the broken computer pieces and started rifling through Elizabeth's desk.

Matt squeezed his hands into angry fists. *Are you the one?* he thought in silent anguish. *Are you the one who killed Julia?*

Elizabeth glanced in the rental car's rearview mirror. "I'm absolutely positive that no one's following us," she said, pressing down on the gas pedal. "There hasn't been a car behind us for at least thirty miles."

Jessica's stomach growled over the blaring

radio. "Does that mean we can finally get something to eat?"

"Sure, but we've got to make it quick." Elizabeth rubbed her bloodshot eyes. They passed a road sign that read Los Angeles 50 miles. "No restaurant this time. We'll have to stop at a convenience store."

"It doesn't matter to me," Jessica said with a yawn. "At this point, the leather sandals I'm wearing are starting to look appetizing."

Elizabeth put on her right-turn signal and pulled into the parking lot of a Gas 'n' Go store. The lot was basically empty, except for a rusty pickup truck filled with fishing equipment in the back. Elizabeth unbuckled her seat belt. "You go on in. I'm going to call Tom." She stepped out of the car. "Remind me to fill up the tank before we go."

Jessica ran inside, and Elizabeth headed for the pay phone near the door. She punched in her calling card number and the number for Tom's room.

The phone rang.

"Please be there, Tom," Elizabeth said aloud. Tom still didn't know they had left the motel last night. She could imagine the horror on his face if he showed up and couldn't find them. Knowing Tom, he'd go on some wild chase trying to locate where they were. At that rate, they'd never hook up.

There was no answer.

After the fifteenth ring, Elizabeth hung up. She

looked at her watch. It was eight thirty. *Maybe he's in my room already*, she thought as she tried again.

"Hello?" Tom answered, picking up the phone on the first ring.

The sound of his voice instantly melted the tension in her neck and shoulders. "Tom, it's me."

"Oh, Liz, I'm so glad to hear from you," he said, sounding relieved. "Did you get any sleep last night?"

Elizabeth bit her lip. "Almost none," she said gravely. "Jessica was hungry, so we went to eat at the motel diner. But some guy in there was staring at us—and I had this really creepy feeling he might've been one of the people after us." Her voice wavered as she told him how they'd crawled out the bathroom window and made a run for it. It all seemed so distant, like a bad dream. "After we sneaked out, it was obvious that we couldn't stick around. We drove around in circles for hours, making sure no one was following us."

Alarm sounded in Tom's voice. "Are you all right? Where are you right now?"

"We're fine," Elizabeth said. "We decided to head toward L.A. It's easier to go unnoticed there."

Jessica stepped out of the store, holding a Double Super Jumbo Guzzler filled with cola and a breakfast burrito. The soda container was about the same diameter as was Jessica's head.

Elizabeth flashed a look of annoyance at her sister. "You could jump in and take a bath in that

136

thing," she said, covering the phone's mouthpiece with her hand.

Jessica stuck out her tongue and took a defiant sip from the long, fat soda straw.

"I have the newspaper articles about New Vision and Mammoth, but for some reason, I can't find your address book," Tom said.

"Are you sure?" Elizabeth asked. "It was on my desk when I left."

"Well, it's not there now," Tom said uneasily. "Maybe someone came back for it."

Elizabeth's knees began to tremble. Whoever was after them seemed to be only one step behind, and getting closer. Doom was descending upon them the same way it would've if they were trapped in an elevator and the air was running out. If she didn't figure out a way to escape this mess soon, they'd both be breathing their last breaths.

"I'm leaving right now," Tom said. "Where should I meet you?"

Elizabeth looked at Jessica. "Where should he meet us?" she asked.

Jessica swallowed a mouthful of soda. "How about the Santa Monica Pier? Near the roller coaster."

"Santa Monica Pier, near the roller coaster," Elizabeth repeated. "How fast can you get there?"

"It'll take me about an hour and a half," Tom said.

"Please hurry," Elizabeth pleaded. Tingling panic started at the nape of her neck and slid down her back to the tip of her spine. "I'm scared, Tom. I have this terrible feeling that something bad is going to happen."

"Don't worry, Liz," the young guy said. From the crack in the closet door, Matt could see him writing on a piece of paper. "The Santa Monica Pier. I'll be there as soon as I can." He hung up the phone.

*Elizabeth Wakefield is going to be at the Santa Monica Pier.* Matt slumped noiselessly against the wall of the closet, heady with the strange feeling of relief. But no sooner did he feel the burden lift from his shoulders than it instantly returned again. Even though Elizabeth held the secret to Julia's murder, the information would be lost if anything happened to her. Kate Morgan was most likely murdered for what she knew, and now Elizabeth could be next.

The door to the room closed, and Matt stepped out of the closet. It would take that guy an hour and a half to get to the Santa Monica Pier, but Matt knew a shortcut that took only an hour. Still, it wasn't much time. But he was determined to get to her before anyone else did.

Matt stood in the middle of the room, wondering if there was anything else he needed. *How am I supposed to find you, Elizabeth, if I don't even know what you look like?* Matt walked over to the bookshelf, a small framed photograph catching his eye. It was a picture of a young, happy couple sitting on a beach blanket, holding hands. The guy in the picture was the same one Matt had seen on the phone a few minutes ago.

"And you must be Elizabeth," he said aloud to the young girl with blond hair and sparkling eyes. There was something familiar about her, in the glowing face and sensitive smile. Matt had the nagging feeling that he'd met her before, but he couldn't place where or when.

"You're the key to my future, Elizabeth," Matt said to the picture, before sliding it into the pocket of his leather jacket. "Please be careful out there."

"I don't feel so well," Jessica said as she handed her last Skee-Ball to Elizabeth. She clutched her stomach dramatically and fell against the nearest pinball machine. "I think I'm going to throw up."

Elizabeth rolled the Skee-Ball straight up the middle of the aisle. The ball hit the hump, then landed precisely in the fifty-point ring. "I have no sympathy for you." Elizabeth collected the string of orange-colored tickets that kept popping out of the machine. "You deserve to feel sick after drinking a gallon container of soda in the car, then insisting on eating a bag of cotton candy once we got here." She curled her lip in revulsion. "You've eaten so much junk, I'm surprised your body hasn't gone into sugar shock."

"It wasn't all junk," Jessica whined. "I had the

breakfast burrito. That had eggs and cheese and sausage and—" She stopped, as if just naming the ingredients were enough to make her nauseous.

Elizabeth rolled her eyes. "Let's cash in our tickets," she said, nodding in the direction of the prize counter. It was hard to be in a bad mood in an arcade. With all the flashing colored lights, the whirring sirens, and suspense in the air, Elizabeth couldn't help but feel a bit festive. She slapped her trail of orange tickets on the glass counter with gusto. "Could you count these up for me, please?"

The man behind the counter took the tickets and fed them through an automatic counter.

"What do you want to get?" Jessica asked.

Elizabeth looked at the prize shelves behind the counter, piled high with funky telephones, remote-control cars, and sleek surfboards. "I don't know. There's so much to choose from."

"See the set of glass mugs on the third shelf from the bottom?" Jessica pointed out. "Santa Monica Pier is etched into each one of them. They're kind of pretty—and they're only 700 tickets."

Elizabeth smiled excitedly. "Before we start making decisions, let's see how many tickets we have."

The man handed Elizabeth a piece of paper with the final tally. "One hundred thirty tickets," he said gruffly.

"That's it?" Jessica blurted out. "I can't believe it,

Liz. And you kept hitting those fifty-pointers, too."

Elizabeth frowned. "What can we get?"

The man behind the counter smiled, pointing down to the bottom of the glass case. "Anything in here," he said.

Jessica and Elizabeth sank to the floor to get a better look. The bottom of the glass case was lined with blue buckets filled with plastic spiders and snakes, penny candy, pencils, kazoos, playing cards, Pogs, glow-in-the-dark tops, and miniature skull key chains.

Jessica sighed. "I say go for the candy. The rest is just junk."

"I think you've had enough candy," Elizabeth answered. "Why don't we go for the cards? It'll keep us busy in those boring motel rooms."

Jessica agreed, and the man handed them a box of cards. They were smaller than average size and had pictures of sea cows on the back of each one. Jessica looked at them distastefully and handed the deck over to her sister. "Skee-Ball is the only game I know where you can spend eight dollars to win a ninety-nine-cent pack of cards."

"Oh, hush!" Elizabeth said, feeling a little guilty about wasting their money on the game. "We had fun, didn't we?"

They turned to leave. As Elizabeth spun around, she bumped into a man who was standing only a foot away from her. Startled, Elizabeth pushed past him, spouting an annoyed, "Excuse me," in his direction.

141

"What was that all about?" Jessica looked back as they stepped out onto the sidewalk.

Elizabeth squinted in the bright, warm sunlight. "I don't know," she said, watching the painted horses on the carousel whizzing by. "Just some creep, I guess," she said dismissively. "Do you want to go on the carousel?"

Jessica rubbed her belly. "Give me an hour or so. I'm still feeling kind of queasy."

They walked past the carousel, the bumper cars, and the fun house, on toward the pier. Elizabeth breathed deeply, taking in the unmistakable combination of fresh, salty ocean air and the heavy, rich scent of frying grease. Childhood memories of carnivals past came rushing back to her, and even though things had seemed grim lately, Elizabeth couldn't help but smile in spite of herself.

"Look, Liz!" Jessica took hold of her sister's wrist and pulled her along. "A fried dough stand!"

Elizabeth's mouth watered instantly. It had been years since she'd bitten into one of those crispy, chewy, golden rounds, slathered with sugar and cinnamon. She looked over at Jessica, whose eyes were glazed with delight, even though she was still holding her aching stomach. "Maybe we should wait a while," Elizabeth said regretfully while the memory still lingered in her mouth. "If you think you're sick now, imagine what it'd be like to have a lump of dough in your stomach. You'd definitely be hating life."

"You're no fun." Jessica pouted. "Why do you always have to be so responsible?"

That was a question Elizabeth had asked herself many times. The only answer she could come up with was that it was a part of her personality; she was born to be responsible. Just like Jessica couldn't help being daring and mischievous, Elizabeth couldn't help wanting to always do what was expected of her. She believed that if you always did what was right, life seemed to go along a lot smoother than for those who didn't. But now she was beginning to wonder if that was true at all.

Elizabeth had taken Professor Zartman's assignment seriously—more seriously than many of the other students—and look where it had gotten her. While the other students were back at campus having fun, Elizabeth was out on the road, running for her life.

Jessica stopped. Her eyes widened suddenly, then narrowed again. "Don't make any sudden moves," she warned. "But look over to the left, near the ringtoss booth. Is that the guy you bumped into at the prize counter?"

Without moving her head, Elizabeth looked out of the corner of her eye. "Yeah, I think so."

"Is he following us?" Jessica's voice was at a higher pitch than usual.

Elizabeth started walking again. "It could be a coincidence," she said calmly. "Let's test it out."

They walked forward a few feet, then took a

sharp right, moving around the tarot card reader's booth. A woman with fake fingernails and a glittery turban beckoned them to have a seat at her table.

"Come, girls, it's only five dollars," the woman said in a thick accent. "I'll tell you all about your future."

*Can you tell me if we'll make it out of here alive?* Elizabeth thought bitterly. Her heart thumped loudly in her ears. They walked quickly, weaving through game booths and food vendors, in a zig-zagging pattern.

They stopped in front of Shoot-the-Duck. "Look around," Elizabeth said breathlessly. "Do you see him?"

Jessica scanned the crowd. "He's over there," she said, sounding on the verge of panic. "I see him standing near the dart game. Liz, he's looking right at us!"

A sudden surge of adrenaline hit Elizabeth. The only thing left to do was to run. "Let's get out of here!"

Grabbing Jessica's hand, Elizabeth pulled her through the crowd. They had to lose him. Without looking back, she plowed ahead, trying to find some place they could go where he couldn't follow. Some place that would buy them a little time.

No sooner did the question cross her mind than an answer followed. The answer was right ahead of them, covered in yellow and blue lights.

"No, Liz. Don't take me on that!" Jessica protested.

"We have to," Elizabeth said as she handed the tickets to the ride operator. "There isn't any time. Besides, he can't see us in here."

They climbed up the steps and walked under a sign that said Gravitron in flashing yellow lights. Through the narrow door, they entered the circular chamber. In the dim light, Elizabeth saw people standing against the wall, holding on to the vertical bars on either side of them.

"Why couldn't you have picked the fun house or something?" Jessica squeaked. She stood in the space next to Elizabeth. "This thing doesn't even have safety belts."

"You'll be fine," Elizabeth said, her own stomach clenching with anxiety. "Just hold on."

The Gravitron started spinning. At first, it didn't seem too bad to Elizabeth; she liked fast rides. Red, blue, yellow, and green lights flashed, creating a soft blur of color. It was like a tie-dyed T-shirt that was constantly changing.

"Oh no!" Jessica moaned.

The Gravitron picked up speed, and the colors seemed to blend into one solid mass. Elizabeth felt her body being pushed flat against the back wall and lifted slightly by the centrifugal force. Her stomach tingled and felt as if it were rising in her throat. It was the same feeling she always had during the steep drops on a roller coaster. Elizabeth tried to open her mouth to scream, but nothing came out.

145

Suddenly, the floor dropped out from underneath them. But Elizabeth didn't move, held firmly in place by the crushing force. *Now I know how it feels to be the little ball on a roulette wheel,* she thought as she miserably waited for the ride to be over.

After a few minutes, the floor moved back into place, and the Gravitron slowed. Elizabeth felt herself sinking to the floor, and for the first time since the ride had gained speed, she was able to move her head. She looked over at Jessica, whose skin had turned a pale green color.

"Are you all right?" Elizabeth asked. The ride came to a complete stop, and she stepped away from the bars.

Jessica nodded. "Actually, I feel a little better," she said, smoothing her hair back into place. "When the ride started up, I got sick."

Elizabeth looked at her sister's dry jeans and halter top. The floor in front of her was clean. "Where did it go?"

"I'm not sure," Jessica said as she looked around. "It's amazing what physics can do."

Looking across the Gravitron from where Jessica was standing, Elizabeth spotted a ten-year-old boy who was covered with a suspicious substance. "I think I've solved the mystery," she said.

They headed for the exit. The ten-year-old boy had a disgusted look on his face. He stared hard at each person in line, as if he'd be able to identify the culprit.

As Jessica and Elizabeth passed, Jessica pinched her nose and looked at him contemptuously. "Whew! Somebody stinks in here!" she said with revulsion. Then she turned away and glided through the door.

"I can't believe it!" Elizabeth sneered under her breath. Her eyes focused on the ice-cream cart directly in front of them. The man who'd been following them earlier was waiting for them to get off the ride.

"What are we going to do?" Jessica gripped her sister's arm. "He's looking right at us."

Elizabeth's mind reeled. They descended the stairs slowly. "When we get to the bottom, run behind the stairs, then around the Gravitron. We really need a distraction, though." Suddenly a brilliant idea came to her. She turned to the ten-year-old with the damp shirt. "Hey, kid. See the guy in the jacket, standing by the ice-cream cart? He's the one who threw up on you."

In a flash, the boy ran down the stairs and headed for the guy. The girls made a break for it. They ran around the Ferris wheel, past the Tilt-o-Whirl, and underneath the Super Slide.

"Let's head for the pier!" Jessica gasped. They ran up the steep wooden steps, flanked by people on all sides. It was the perfect place to get lost.

The spicy smell of oregano and garlic wafted through the air as they dodged past the Pier Pizzeria. Beyond the restaurant were vendor booths, selling custom-made airbrushed

T-shirts and personalized license plates. They kept on running, the wooden boards pounding underfoot.

"Stop right there," a man said, blocking their entrance to the bar at the end of the pier. "I need to see some ID."

Elizabeth looked back worriedly. "We just want to use the bathroom."

"You can't go in here unless you're twenty-one," the bouncer said. "Use the bathroom at the Pier Pizzeria."

Elizabeth slumped on the nearest bench. "Maybe we lost him," she panted.

"Where are we going to go? We're at the end of the pier!" Jessica's voice shrilled.

"We just have to sit here and wait, and hope for the best." There were hundreds of people on the pier; how could he possibly find them in the crowd?

As soon as the thought crossed her mind, Elizabeth glanced up to see the man pushing through the crowd, coming directly toward them. His gait was purposeful and determined. Even though he was wearing sunglasses, Elizabeth could feel the heat of his eyes boring holes through her.

Jessica clutched Elizabeth's arm. Her hands were cold and shaking. "He's coming for us!"

"Stay calm," Elizabeth directed, even though her insides were one big trembling mess. "We'll talk our way out of it."

The man stopped directly in front of them. His mustache was damp with sweat. Looking down at them, he reached inside his jacket pocket. "Okay, girls," he said evenly. "The chase is over."

# Chapter Ten

Jessica squeezed her eyes shut and hid her head behind Elizabeth's shoulder, waiting for the inevitable crackle of gunfire. *This is it,* she thought with numbing terror. *We're going to die.*

"I've been trying to find you for a few days now," he said with a laugh. "And I've finally got you cornered."

"What do you want from us?" Elizabeth shouted defiantly.

Jessica opened her eyes. The man reached into his jacket and pulled out a picture frame. He handed it to Elizabeth. "I took that off your desk so I'd know what you looked like."

Elizabeth tightly held the picture of her and Tom. "Are you the person who broke into my room and smashed my computer?"

"No, no—," he said, shaking his head. "I'm here because I have reason to believe you know something about Julia Reynolds's death. I need to know everything."

Elizabeth aggressively folded her arms across her chest. "I don't know what you're talking about."

Following her twin's lead, Jessica leaned back on the bench and yawned in feigned boredom. "Who's Julia Reynolds?"

The man's mouth drew back into a taut line. "So that's how it is," he said through gritted teeth. "I thought you might know who the killers were, but now it looks like you two were in on it the whole time." He leaned over them, blocking out the sun. "Well, don't worry, I'll see to it that you get yours."

Jessica bit her cheek to hold back a scream.

"You don't fool me at all," Elizabeth spat out. "This is just a ploy. We're not going to admit anything."

The man took off his sunglasses and slipped them into the front pocket of his leather jacket. Jessica stared with fright into his amber-colored eyes. There was something about those eyes that were familiar.

*Where have I seen you before?* Her gazed traveled along the strong line of his bearded chin and up to his long brown hair.

"In the cemetery!" she blurted out impulsively. "I met you in the cemetery a few days ago at Julia Reynolds's grave!"

Elizabeth looked completely confused.

"What are you talking about?" she asked incredulously.

The man peered down at her, then a vague smile crossed his face. "I remember you," he said. "You were the one crying. You said Julia meant the world to you."

Jessica nodded furiously. "That was me!" she shouted. "I was really worried about you. I thought you'd do something drastic."

"Would someone please tell me what's going on?" Elizabeth insisted.

Jessica waved in the man's direction. "This man is one of Julia's biggest fans," she said. Jessica extended her hand to him. "We never officially met. I'm Jessica Wakefield, and this is my sister, Elizabeth."

The man shook Jessica's hand, but Elizabeth refused. "It's a pleasure to meet both of you," he said. "I'm Matt Barron."

Jessica's jaw dropped. *Did I hear right?* Her heart stopped. Jessica studied his face, comparing every feature with the image inside her head. Mentally, she shaved off the beard and mustache. In an instant she was hit with a lightning bolt of recognition.

Elizabeth reached out to shake his hand. "I'm so sorry, Mr. Barron," she said apologetically. "It's nice to meet you."

"Please, call me Matt." He took a seat on the bench next to Jessica.

Matt brushed against Jessica's arm, leaving a

tingling sensation that crawled all the way up to her neck. *Close your mouth, Jess, you're drooling.* Jessica silently hoped she didn't smell like vomit. If she had known she'd meet Matt Barron today, she never would've had the Double Super Jumbo Guzzler, and she definitely would've made Elizabeth pull over at a roadside hair salon.

"I need your help," Matt said seriously. Puffy half-moons darkened the area under his eyes. "I know Julia didn't kill herself, and I'm trying to find out who did. A woman named Kate Morgan told me she had some information. But before she could fill me in on it, she was murdered."

*If only Lila and Isabella were here to see this!* Jessica tried to stay focused on the conversation, but all she could think about was how much better Matt looked in person than on the big screen.

"I know about Kate Morgan," Elizabeth whispered.

Matt leaned in closer, his shoulder touching Jessica's. Her heart felt as if it were about to explode. *I can't believe it!* she thought mindlessly. *Matt Barron is leaning against me.* Jessica wasn't afraid anymore of being hunted by assassins. If she had to die at this very moment, she'd die a happy woman.

"What do you know?" Matt asked intently.

Jessica boldly touched Matt's elbow. "I've seen all your movies," she whispered. "And a moment ago, when I said 'Julia who?' I was just kidding. She's my idol."

Matt smiled graciously. "I have to know every-thing," he said to Elizabeth.

Elizabeth leaned over Jessica, pushing her even closer to Matt. "I wrote a research paper for my journalism class, outlining a theory I had about a possible conspiracy. At the time, I thought the whole idea was pretty ridiculous, but now I think I hit it right on the mark."

"Tell me all about it," Matt said, shaking his silky hair.

Jessica got a whiff of his cologne. It had a musky, woody scent. *It must be imported,* she thought dreamily.

"I have to warn you," Elizabeth said in a grave tone. "Everyone who's read my paper is dead. And I have a strong suspicion that I'm next."

"It doesn't matter." Matt reached across Jessica's lap and touched Elizabeth's hand. "Tell me everything."

"Thanks for getting these for me," Elizabeth said, taking the folder of newspaper clippings from Tom and setting it on the hotel bureau.

Tom scanned the hotel room. "This place looks a little better than the last one."

Elizabeth plopped down on a green uphol-stered chair. "We decided to spring a little extra for a nicer room. After all, this is our home for a while." She held up her leather-bound address book. "I got my book back. Matt had it the whole time."

154

Tom touched Elizabeth's face. "I don't want to leave you again."

"You have to. If anyone sees us together, you'll be in danger, too," Elizabeth insisted, looking deeply into Tom's brown eyes. "Besides, we need you at SVU doing research. Jessica and I can take care of ourselves."

"I have no doubt about that." Tom kissed Elizabeth on the forehead. "I'm just worried about leaving you alone with a handsome celebrity."

Elizabeth stood up and wrapped her arms around Tom's neck. "Why would I want a handsome celebrity when I have the best guy in the whole world?" She gave Tom a long, slow, lingering kiss that left them both feeling weak. "Besides, I think Jessica already has her sights on Matt Barron."

On the other side of the room, Jessica was busy molding her hair into a glamorous pile on top of her head. She posed provocatively for the mirror, pouting her lips like a runway model. "Liz, why didn't you pack my hair curlers?" Jessica whined.

Elizabeth and Tom laughed, walking arm in arm toward the door. "Call me if anything happens," Tom said firmly. "Anything at all."

"I will." Elizabeth smiled, kissing him lightly on the lips. "I'm going to miss you."

Tom's eyes looked sad. "I'm going to miss you, too. Don't try to do anything brave, Liz. Just keep yourself safe."

She blew him a kiss, then closed the door. *I hope this thing blows over soon,* she thought grimly. *I miss having a normal life.*

Suddenly, there was a knock at the door. Elizabeth peered through the peephole and smiled.

"I thought you'd left," she said, opening the door.

Tom cupped her face in his hands. "Did I tell you I love you?"

"A million times. But you can say it again." Elizabeth pressed her lips against Tom's, melting in his kiss.

"That's so you won't forget me," he said. Then he turned and walked down the hallway.

Elizabeth sighed contentedly. She leaned against the door, and instantly there was another knock. Elizabeth whipped around and yanked the door open again. "What is it this—" She stopped short.

But it wasn't Tom. Elizabeth jumped back. "Oh no!" she shrieked.

"Do I really look that bad?" Matt asked, looking nearly as frightened.

"No," Elizabeth said, catching her breath. "I thought you were . . ."

Matt walked into the room. "That's it," he said scratching at his beard. "I'm shaving this thing off."

For the first time since they'd arrived at the hotel, Jessica turned away from the mirror and skipped over to the door. "Matt, it's good to see you again," she said coolly. "Excuse my sister, she doesn't know how to properly greet guests."

Elizabeth shot Jessica a haughty look. "I was expecting my boyfriend, that's all."

The corners of Matt's mouth turned up in amusement. "It's okay, I understand. But you shouldn't open the door without looking through the peephole first."

Jessica shook her head. "I've told her a thousand times. She never listens."

"Would you like to have a seat?" Elizabeth said, forcing a smile.

Jessica ran over to the sink. "Let me get you some water."

Matt smiled, tucking a strand of hair behind his ear. "I've been thinking about 'The Suicide Paper,' and I think your theory is right on the money. Mammoth had all the motive in the world to kill Julia. Not only did she break her contract, but her history of depression made it the perfect cover-up."

Elizabeth's ponytail bobbed as she nodded in agreement. "Plus she was starring in New Vision's summer blockbuster," she said. "Ronald Bishop was probably afraid that Mammoth wouldn't be able to compete. If his company started losing money, people would start delving into the numbers, trying to figure out why."

"And that's when they'd begin to see that Bishop was skimming a little off the top to support his gambling debts," Matt added.

Jessica put a Pacific Hotel coaster in front of Matt and set a glass of ice water on top of it. Then she quietly took a seat at the table.

"Thanks," Matt said, taking a sip.

Elizabeth rested her elbows on the tabletop. "The only way Bishop could save himself would be to make sure New Vision goes bankrupt. And the easiest way to do that would be to sabotage New Vision's summer movie by killing off its star."

Matt thought quietly for a moment, pressing his fingertips against his forehead. "The only problem is, New Vision would have to lose more than one movie to go bankrupt."

Elizabeth's eyes narrowed. "How many would it take?"

"I don't know for sure. At least two, possibly more."

Jessica flipped her hair over one shoulder. "Are you saying they could kill another actress?"

"At this point, nothing would surprise me," Matt said sourly.

Elizabeth's blue-green eyes glazed over as the pieces started to come together. "That's why they're after us. They want to shut us up so they can carry out the rest of the plot." Thoughts spun wildly in her mind, pressing down on her with increased urgency. "Matt, who else has broken a contract with Mammoth to go to New Vision?"

Matt took another sip of water. "The only one I

can think of offhand is Candice Johannsen. But she didn't actually break a contract with Mammoth. She said she'd star in their summer romance, but at the last minute she backed out of the deal and went to New Vision." He nodded slowly as if everything were beginning to make perfect sense. "They're filming the movie right now. Candice would be the perfect target. . . . She's a recovering drug addict. They could make her death look like a suicide, too."

"We have to warn her," Elizabeth said emphatically. "She could be next."

Matt's perfectly shaped lips twisted in thought. "The best thing to do would be to go to the set tomorrow and tell her," he said. "But Candice and Julia never hit it off. She'd think I was just trying to scare her. Someone else has to do it."

Jessica nearly jumped out of her chair. "Me!" she shouted. "I'll go! I'll do it!"

Matt chuckled. "Do you think you can handle the cutthroat movie industry?"

Elizabeth pursed her lips. "You obviously don't know Jessica very well."

Matt's beeper went off. He unclipped it from his belt and looked curiously at the number. "I don't recognize this one," he said. "Do you mind if I use the phone?"

"Go right ahead." Elizabeth gestured to the nightstand.

While Matt dialed the number, Jessica leaned toward Elizabeth, her eyes sparkling. "I can't believe this!" she whispered with giddy excitement. "It's a dream come true!"

"This isn't a game, Jess!" Elizabeth countered. "People's lives are at stake—including ours."

"So what if we're in danger? Can't we make the most of it?" Jessica put her hands firmly on her hips. "It's not every day that we're on the run with a gorgeous movie star. And it's not every day that I get to stroll onto a movie set!"

Elizabeth rubbed her temples. "I wish you'd take things a bit more seriously."

Jessica scowled. "You are *so* negative."

Matt hung up the phone. The lines that creased his forehead earlier were beginning to fade. "That was a man named Gomez. He said he has some important information. He's going to meet us by the waterfront under the bridge tomorrow night."

Elizabeth's brow furrowed. "Are you sure we're not being set up?"

Matt shook his head. "He's for real," he said gravely. "The only thing I'm afraid of is that he'll back out."

"Here's your studio pass." Matt handed Jessica a laminated card with New Vision Studios printed in rainbow colors across the top. He pointed down the block to the guard's station. "It'll get you through the front gates. The rest you'll have to finesse."

Jessica shoved the pass into the pocket of her

jeans. She frowned, looking down at her sneakers and white T-shirt. "Are you sure I shouldn't be wearing something more glamorous?"

Elizabeth sighed. "You're only pretending to be an extra, not the leading lady."

"What would you know about Hollywood?" Jessica asked. She turned to Matt. "Am I underdressed?"

Matt gave her a wink. "You look great." He took his sunglasses off. "If it'll make you feel more glamorous, you can wear my shades."

Jessica squealed with delight. "They're Vito Bertoluccis! Imported from Italy!" She slid the sunglasses on luxuriously.

"Actually, I bought them in Rome." Matt smiled.

Elizabeth rolled her eyes. "Can we go over the game plan?"

"Right." Matt suddenly grew serious. "If anyone stops you once you're inside the gates, just tell them you're an extra for the movie *Forbidden Desire*. They'll tell you where you should go."

"You need to be on the lookout for Candice Johannsen the whole time," Elizabeth added. "As soon as you warn her, you have to get off the lot immediately. We can't afford to have you discovered."

Matt ran a hand through his hair. "The key to dealing with Hollywood types is to constantly give off an air of bored superiority. For the really tough ones, turn on the charm."

161

Elizabeth kissed Jessica on the cheek. "You'll be perfect," she said proudly. "Go break a leg."

"And one more thing," Matt said, handing Jessica a set of black car keys. "You'll be needing these."

"Oh, thank you!" Jessica frantically embraced Matt.

"This is a mission, not a birthday present," Elizabeth said dryly.

Matt stumbled, trying to regain his balance. "Take good care of my car."

"I will," Jessica promised coyly as she slipped into the driver's seat of Matt's black Ferrari. She turned the key, and the engine roared. "Bye, now." With a graceful wave, she tore down the road.

*I've got the car and the sunglasses, who could ever doubt that I belong on a movie set?* Jessica's stomach fluttered. Deep down, she had a feeling this was going to be the biggest day of her life.

Even though it was only a block away, the entrance to New Vision Studios came up a lot quicker than Jessica had anticipated. She slammed on the brakes, bringing the speeding sports car to a screeching halt. Jessica pictured Matt down the road grinding his beautiful white teeth in agony. Carefully, she turned into the entrance gate.

"Pass, please, ma'am," the stern-looking guard said.

Jessica tipped her sunglasses down a fraction and smiled as she handed him the card. "Is there a problem?"

"No, ma'am," the guard said. "What movie set are you working on?"

"*Forbidden Desire.*" She mouthed the words seductively, in her best Marilyn Monroe impersonation.

The guard opened the gate. "That movie is shooting on lot fourteen."

Jessica pushed her sunglasses higher on her nose. "I *know*," she said patronizingly. Facing straight ahead, she slammed down on the gas pedal and tore onto the studio lot.

"Yippee!" Jessica screamed. In a matter of minutes, she would be rubbing elbows with directors, makeup artists, actors. Her stomach churned with excitement. Following the arrows to lot fourteen, Jessica parked in one of the spaces outside the building.

Jessica sauntered across the lot. She kept her mouth in a full, disapproving pout and tilted her head to the side and up, to maintain a proper look of superiority. But behind the sunglasses, Jessica's eyes were as wide as tidal pools, drinking in the atmosphere.

People scampered in all directions, some dressed in costume, others in white T-shirts and baseball caps bearing the New Vision logo. Thick electrical cords trailed from lighting equipment; props were being shuffled from one end of the set to another. Everyone seemed so wrapped up in their own duties that no one noticed Jessica at all.

*This is a piece of cake,* Jessica thought with pride

163

as she wandered over to the movie trailers. Facing forward, Jessica scanned the names on the trailers out of the corner of her eye.

At last, she found Candice's trailer.

Jessica eyed the small metal trailer with longing. There were two narrow windows at each end, the blinds closed tight. On the door, the name *Candice Johannsen* was stenciled in gold script letters. And above that, there was a shiny gold star.

*I wonder what she keeps in there.* Only a flimsy metal door kept Jessica from finding out all the delicious secrets of one of Hollywood's hottest stars. Candice, who had been married several times, probably kept photo albums of all her famous lovers, not to mention all the romantic letters each one of them had sent. Candice's dressing trailer was probably brimming with exotic objects from around the world. Jessica gasped, trying to imagine the fantastic makeup kit that sat on top of Candice's vanity. She probably owned the entire spectrum of lipstick shades from luminous oyster pearl to mulled brandywine.

*I'll just take a quick peek.* Jessica took a fast look around as she started up the stairs. No one seemed to notice. She reached for the door handle. *What harm is there in looking?* Jessica rationalized. *After all, I may never be on a movie set again.*

"Excuse me, miss," a voice boomed behind her.

Visions of Candice's lipstick collection scattered like translucent powder on a dry makeup brush. She hadn't been on the set more than ten minutes, and already Jessica was being kicked off. She turned on her heels. "Yes?" Jessica said in her most affected tone.

"Miss, are you an extra?" the young man sporting a clean New Vision baseball cap asked.

*Actually, I'm a spy,* Jessica thought to herself. *And a bad one at that.* She smiled brightly. "Am I in the wrong place?"

"Well, yeah," the young man said. "The extras are supposed to be by the studio entrance over there."

"Stupid me!" Jessica's smile froze solid on her face while she waited in nervous anticipation for the security guards to come over and handcuff her. "I guess I should head over there then," she said testily.

"If you don't mind, please stay right where you are." The young man looked her up and down. "The director would like to use you for a walk-on part."

Flames of frenzied delight burned like a furnace inside Jessica while her exterior maintained a cool, even temperature. She lifted her head slightly and looked down her nose as she said with icy detachment, "Whatever the director wants."

"Turn your head to the left, please." The plump hairdresser smiled at Jessica in the mirror as she unclipped the last hot roller. "You have beautiful hair."

Jessica beamed. "Thank you," she said, blushing. "I deep condition at least once a week." *Thank goodness I didn't let Elizabeth dye our hair.*

"It shows. Your hair is like silk." The hairdresser ran her fingers through the curls, coaxing them to fall softly around Jessica's shoulders.

A tall man with a pointed nose and a buzz cut sidled up to the hairdresser. "Makeup time, sweetie."

The hairdresser pulled Jessica's hair back into a loose chignon, letting corkscrew curls cascade from either side of her face. "All done," the hairdresser said.

"Thank you," Jessica said gratefully.

The hairdresser smiled. "My pleasure." She patted the makeup artist on the shoulder. "See you around, Martin."

Martin wheeled the makeup cart in front of Jessica. "You'd better hurry, Helen," he said to the hairdresser in a singsong voice. "Candice is waiting for you in her trailer."

Helen smirked. "Candice can keep on waiting, as far as I'm concerned."

Martin smiled with delight as he turned his attention to Jessica. "How are *you* today, sweetie?"

"Wonderful!" Jessica said, no longer able to maintain her cool facade. "This is so much fun!"

"Glad you're having a good time," Martin said, pumping the chair up higher. "If you did this every day, it would get boring just like everything else."

"Wait a sec, Martin!" a woman shouted from across the room. She lunged toward Jessica with pieces of fabric in her hand and a cloth measuring tape draped around her neck. "Before you start, I need to pick out a color."

Martin stepped aside. "This is Sheryl from wardrobe. She's always in a hurry."

"What do you think of this color?" Sheryl asked, holding a swatch of grapey purple cloth against Jessica's face.

Martin lifted his pointy nose in the air. "No, no . . . it washes her out." He picked an orange-red swatch out of the pile. "This one's nice."

"Can't do it," Sheryl said. "Candice is wearing robin's egg blue. When they stand next to each other, it's going to clash." She pulled a forest green swatch out of the pile, tucking it under Jessica's chin. "How about this?"

"That's the one," Martin cooed. "Sweetie would look absolutely divine in that color."

Sheryl nodded vigorously as she headed out the door. "I'll be right back."

Martin took out a huge powder brush and began dusting Jessica's face. "Didn't I tell you that woman was always in a hurry? Rush, rush, rush!" He tilted Jessica's chin up toward the light, then smiled. "I can see I won't have much work to do on this lovely face!"

Jessica closed her eyes and eased back into the chair while Martin worked on her face. *I'm getting a makeover by a professional artist . . . on a movie*

*set. I'm doing a scene with Candice Johannsen.* . . .
*I'm going to be in a movie.* . . . *I'm going to be famous.* . . . Thoughts ricocheted in Jessica's mind like ball bearings in a pinball machine. Everything was happening so fast, Jessica was afraid it would all slip away like a dream.

She quickly opened her eyes and was grateful to see that nothing had changed.

"Aaah!" Martin yelped, yanking his arm back. "Keep your eyes closed, sweetie! You almost got an eye full of mascara!"

"Sorry," Jessica apologized, closing her eyes again. She heard the low, mournful squeak of the trailer door opening, then slamming shut.

"Jessica Monroe?"

"She's over here!" Martin called, tracing the outline of Jessica's lips with liner pencil.

An energetic woman with a VIP pass hanging from a chain around her neck pulled up a stool and sat next to Jessica. "Hi, Jessica, my name is Jodie. I'm going to guide you through your scene." Jodie spoke in a quick and precise manner, giving Jessica the feeling that she'd better listen closely, because nothing would be repeated.

"We're on a tight schedule today, Jessica," Jodie said. She handed Jessica a sheet of paper. "These are your lines. We'll be shooting in twenty minutes."

Jessica held the paper up to the light, as Martin carefully painted lipstick on her mouth. Her head was tilted at an awkward angle, making it difficult to read the page. Eventually she gave up, dropping the paper in her lap.

"Let me set the scene for you," Jodie said abruptly. "You'll be acting with the two stars, Candice Johannsen and Mason Avery Thomas. It takes place in a posh restaurant, where Candice and Mason—Julie and Edgar in the script—are having a candlelit dinner. Julie, who's just fallen in love with her aerobics instructor, is about to break it off with Edgar. Edgar, on the other hand, has just come to terms with the death of his first wife and realizes that he's been neglecting Julie. He hopes it's not too late to save their relationship, and in a fit of passion, he proposes to her." Jodie stopped to take a deep breath. "Got all that?"

Jessica's head was swimming. She nodded absently as Martin blotted her lips.

"You play the part of the waitress," Jodie continued. "Right after Edgar proposes, you come in, say your line, then leave. The details are in the script I just gave you." Jodie stood up. "If you don't have any questions, I'll see you on the set in ten minutes."

Hundreds of questions buzzed around Jessica's head like a swarm of angry bees. She opened her mouth to ask Jodie a question, but Martin started slathering her lips with gloss.

"Hold still, sweetie," Martin said. Before Jessica had a chance to stop her, Jodie was already out the door.

"How much longer?" Jessica asked, her voice

tinged with anxiety. At the rate things were going, she'd be lucky to have five minutes to learn her part.

Martin took a step back and surveyed his work. "Just a few touch-ups here and there." His hand fluttered in the air as if he were painting an invisible canvas. "Then Sheryl should be here to fit you for your costume."

Jessica swallowed hard.

"Don't you worry about a thing, sweetie," Martin said brightly. "You're a natural."

"Places, everybody!" The director cupped her hands on either side of her mouth and shouted into the air. "Places!"

Jessica stood to the left of the set, her knees trembling uncontrollably. The green apron Sheryl had picked out had been too big, so they'd had to pin it in the back. As if she weren't edgy enough, Jessica was now afraid to move because the slightest turn in the wrong direction might jab a pin into her side.

*Where am I supposed to be?* Jessica watched timidly as the camera crew and actors took off in all different directions. Grasping the script in her shaking hands, Jessica worked on memorizing her part.

"Okay, so Edgar proposes to Julie . . ." Jessica paced back and forth, talking the scene out. "Then I say, 'Is it satisfactory, sir?'" Jessica whipped around, ignoring the pin that poked painfully into her side. "That doesn't make any sense. This whole thing doesn't make any sense!"

Hot tears clouded her eyes. *Don't cry now. Please don't cry now.* Jessica fanned herself with the script, hoping to stop the tears from ruining her mascara. *How completely unprofessional, Jessica Wakefield. You haven't been on the set for more than three minutes, and already you're crying.*

"But I don't know when to come in or when to leave!" she argued aloud with the voice inside her head. How could a one-line part seem so incredibly difficult? A million and one questions still raged inside her head, and if they weren't answered, Jessica knew she was going to make a complete idiot of herself in front of the most important people in Hollywood. With every tortured moment that passed, Jessica became more and more certain that she wasn't cut out for the movie business.

"Okay, everybody, listen up!" the director yelled. "Candice and Mason are going to do a quick read-through before we get the cameras rolling. It shouldn't take too long, so be ready."

*If I only knew what to be ready for,* Jessica thought miserably. This was supposed to be the most exciting moment of her life, and all she could think about was what a disaster it was going to be.

Mason walked onto the elaborate set and took a seat at the table. The set was made to look like an expensive Italian restaurant, with white tablecloths and plasticware that looked like fine silver

171

and expensive china. There were rubber potted trees around them and candles on each table. Fake artwork lined the walls. In the corner of the room, there was even a grand piano made out of painted Styrofoam that looked frighteningly real.

Even though the walls of the set restaurant were actually made out of flimsy plywood and all the props were fake, Mason sat with a suave sophistication that suggested he was truly dining at the finest restaurant in Italy. Jessica immediately sensed that she was in the presence of a fine actor.

A moment later, Candice stumbled onto the set and took the seat opposite Mason. Jessica's heart sank with disappointment at the sight of the legendary movie star. She looked at least ten times older than she did on-screen. *So that's what drugs do to a person,* Jessica thought with pity. Deep lines that even makeup couldn't erase creased Candice's forehead and cheeks. Her usually lush brunette hair seemed dull and mousy in person. Unlike Mason's debonair quality, Candice brought to the set a vague sadness. She seemed just as fake as the props around her.

*"You need to be on the lookout for Candice Johannsen the whole time,"* Elizabeth's voice echoed in Jessica's head. *"People's lives are at stake—including ours."* In the flurry of activity, Jessica had nearly forgotten the real reason why she was on the set in the first place. *As soon as the scene is over,* Jessica vowed, *I'll warn her.*

"Excuse me, Ms. Monroe."

Jessica was snapped out of her reverie by a middle-aged man in a New Vision windbreaker. He was carrying a cardboard box full of props.

"Yes?" she said.

The man motioned for her to follow him around to the back of the restaurant set. "My name is Don," he said. "I brought the props you'll need for the scene."

Jessica stared hopelessly at the box. There was a corkscrew, a bottle of red wine, and two wine-glasses. Tears welled up in her eyes for a second time. She didn't have the faintest idea about what to do with any of those things.

Don handed her the bottle of wine. He reached down to pick up the glasses, when suddenly he stopped and looked at Jessica. "Why so glum?"

"I don't know what I'm doing," Jessica sobbed. She furiously fanned her eyes to keep them dry. "I have this stupid waitress part that a two-year-old could learn, and I know I'm going to ruin everything."

"Now, now—take it easy." Don handed Jessica a handkerchief. "First of all, there is no such thing as a stupid role. Every role in a performance is important. No matter what the part is, if you take it out, something is definitely missing from the overall meaning of the movie."

Jessica scoffed. "Come on, Don. I have one measly line. It doesn't mean that much."

"Let me take a look at that," Don said, reaching

for the script. He pulled a pair of black reading glasses out of his jacket pocket and looked over the scene. Every few lines he nodded, then hummed to himself, like a schoolteacher grading an essay.

After a moment or two, Don folded up his glasses and returned them to his pocket. "This is no small part, my dear," he said finally.

Jessica eyed him skeptically, the corner of her mouth turning up in a half smile. "What makes you say that?"

Don raised his eyebrows as if the reasons were too many to count. "First of all, this is the most important scene in the movie. Whether or not Julie accepts Edgar's proposal is pivotal—her answer decides the fate of both characters."

Jessica listened closely, occasionally dabbing at her eyes to make sure her mascara wasn't streaking down her face.

Don continued. "Now, right after Edgar proposes, when the audience is on the edge of their seats waiting to hear Julie's answer, you come in." He gestured dramatically to emphasize his point. Jessica leaned closer, hanging on his every word.

"Your part is absolutely crucial," Don said with total seriousness. "And timing is the key. There's a lot riding on this moment. Your character's function is to give Julie a moment to think about Edgar's proposal. Don't linger too long, or the moment will be lost. At the same time, you must be fluid and graceful—not rushed."

Jessica breathed deeply. "I had no idea there

was so much to it. I don't think I can carry it off."

"Of course you can." His voice was more commanding than encouraging. "The secret is to get into the head of your character. You must think like a waitress."

"Think like a waitress?" Jessica repeated.

"Certainly," Don said. "Some of the greatest actors who ever lived used to make up stories about the backgrounds of their characters—everything from what their favorite colors were to the names of their first cousins."

"Wow!" Jessica felt the tight knots in her stomach loosening. "I never thought of it that way."

"Give it a try." Don handed her the wine bottle, corkscrew, and glasses.

At the front of the set, the director was shouting at the crew. "Extras, take your places!" A group of people, who were supposed to be the restaurant patrons, hurried onto the set, filling in the empty seats.

"Wait—" Jessica was suddenly stricken with panic. She looked down at the props in her hands. "I still don't know what to do with all this stuff, Don. Is there someone who can help me?"

Don touched Jessica's forehead lightly. A wave of calm seemed to pass from his fingertips through her. "Everything you need to know is in here." Then he pointed to the door on the right-hand side of the restaurant set. "You enter through there when they give you the signal."

Jessica took a deep breath. "Okay. So all I have

to do is pretend I'm a waitress and I'll know exactly what to do?"

Don smiled and nodded. "Go ahead now. They're waiting for you."

Jessica turned and stood by the swinging door, waiting for the scene to begin. Her arms were clasped tightly to her chest, struggling to hold all the props at once. *How would a waitress carry all this stuff?* Jessica tucked the corkscrew into the pocket of her apron and leaned the bottle of wine against the inside of her right forearm, supporting the bottom with her fingers. She hung the two wineglasses upside down, the stems slipped in between the fingers of her left hand. Jessica draped a linen napkin she found in Don's box over her arm for a finishing touch, just like the waiters she'd seen in expensive restaurants.

A lump caught in Jessica's throat, and her mouth went dry. *Don't blow it, Jess. This is your big break.* Her hands started to perspire, making the wineglasses slide along her fingers. *What if I break a glass in the middle of the scene?* Jessica thought in horror. So many things could go wrong. *I could spill red wine all over Mason's lap . . . the cork could get stuck in the bottle . . . I could trip and break my leg in front of everybody.* The possibilities were endless. But the worst thing of all would be if she forgot her line.

For the past several minutes, Jessica's line had been firmly committed to memory. In her mind, she had visualized herself writing it over and over again on a huge chalkboard. But now, as the tension was bearing down on her, she visualized a gigantic eraser, wiping out everything until her mind was completely blank.

*What am I supposed to say?* Jessica struggled to remember her line, but the words eluded her.

"Jessica!" Don whispered loudly. She turned her head to see him motioning to a man on the other side of the set. It was a member of the crew, who was cuing her to enter.

Jessica turned her back and pushed through the swinging door. *Think like a waitress . . . think like a waitress.* As she passed from the backstage reality to the fantasy world of the movie set, a strange transformation took place. Jessica's palms were dry again, and her pulse slowed considerably. She was no longer an awkward, nervous college student. In a fraction of a second, she had become a waitress at a fancy Italian restaurant.

Jessica glided through the maze of dinner tables with grace and ease, as though she had done it a million times before. The man at table four had ordered a bottle of house red. Arriving at the table, she presented the bottle for his inspection and set the wineglasses on the table. With a flourish, she uncorked the bottle and poured a small amount of the dark red liquid into a glass for the man to taste. He took a sip, and as if it were second nature to ask, Jessica said, "Is it satisfactory, sir?"

*That was it! You did it!* Jessica congratulated

herself. Never in her life had anything she'd done felt so right, so perfectly natural. If there was only one thing in life Jessica could be certain about, it was this: She was born to act.

Suddenly Candice stood up, her face looking even more hollow and pale than before. "Stop everything!" she shouted.

Jessica backed away from the table.

The director got up from her chair. "What's wrong?"

Candice sneered. "It's *her*!" She pointed to Jessica. "The blonde has to go!"

Jessica's stomach plummeted like a runaway elevator falling down a shaft. She'd remembered her lines and made her marks—what could have gone wrong?

"I could do it a different way if you want," she suggested to the director.

"Everybody, take five," the director called as she pulled Candice aside.

Mason dropped his dinner napkin on the table impatiently. "You did a fine job," he said in his irresistible English accent. "It's not you, it's *her*."

Jessica watched nervously out of the corner of her eye. Candice was throwing her hands up in the air theatrically and bulging her eyes for effect.

"What's wrong with her?" Jessica whispered to Mason.

Mason toyed with the stem of his wineglass. "Insecurity," he said. "It's a common affliction among aging stars. They can't stand to be in the same room with anyone younger or more beautiful than themselves."

The director put her arm around Candice in an obvious effort to calm her down. Still, Candice was ranting wildly, clutching at her throat as if she were choking on a piece of filet mignon.

Mason watched the scene with a look of disgust. "Why did my agent ever convince me to take this picture? I should've known better than to work with a maniac like her." He eyed the bottle of wine that Jessica was still clutching in her hands. "Would you mind giving me a hit of that?" he said.

Jessica looked around to see if anyone was watching. "Are you sure? I mean, should you be drinking on the job?"

Mason held up his glass. "It's just cranberry juice."

Jessica laughed and poured him some.

"Okay, that's it," the director said, throwing her hands up in a gesture of surrender. "Would someone please escort Ms. Monroe off the set?"

Jessica threw off the apron. Two security guards came by and led her out by the arms, as if she were a criminal who'd been arrested. "Right this way, ma'am."

Just like that, it was over. As she walked back to the parking lot, Jessica imagined that her career was like a shooting star. One moment, it was burning bright and full of promise. The next, it was crashing to earth, hurling through space, and in a blinding flash, it disappeared into the atmosphere.

# Chapter
# Eleven

The black Ferrari squealed into the parking lot where Elizabeth and Matt were waiting. Jessica raced the car over a speed bump, the rear end scraping the bottom with a loud, metallic thud.

Matt flinched.

"I hope you have car insurance," Elizabeth said, covering her eyes.

"It's all right," Matt said. And he meant it. If it had been anyone else, he probably would've been upset. But this was Jessica. In the short time he'd known her, Matt had grown fond of Jessica's unbridled enthusiasm and vitality. Her exuberance was a sharp contrast to the black void in Matt's heart. She bubbled over with life, and he prayed that nothing would ever happen to change her. Matt wanted Jessica to stay exactly the way she was, even if that meant his Ferrari would get a few scrapes and dents along the way.

"Watch out!" Jessica yelled out the window. She honked the horn a few times, then drove straight for the spot where Matt and Elizabeth were standing.

Matt jumped back suddenly, pulling Elizabeth with him. The Ferrari whizzed by, missing them both by a narrow two inches.

"Forget car insurance," Elizabeth said, glaring at the car as it came to a squealing halt. "I hope you have health insurance, too."

Jessica got out of the car. "That is a performance machine!" she said energetically, tossing the keys to Matt.

"I'm glad you like it," he said with a grin. The late afternoon sun played off Jessica's hair, making it look like spun gold. "So how did it go?"

Jessica leaned heavily against the car and handed Matt his Vito Bertolucci sunglasses. All the excitement and sparkle that had been in her beautiful eyes two hours ago was gone. "The whole thing was a big flop."

Elizabeth's shoulders slumped. "I guess you didn't get to see Candice."

"Oh, I saw her all right!" Jessica sneered. "That woman has a serious attitude problem."

Matt shook his head. "Candice does have a reputation for being difficult."

"So did you warn her or not?" Elizabeth asked bluntly.

Jessica twisted a golden strand of hair around

her finger. "I didn't get a chance to. She had me kicked off the set."

Rocking back and forth on her heels, Elizabeth looked as if she were about to explode. A flood of color rushed to her cheeks. "All you had to do was go in there and warn her. What did you do to mess things up?"

Jessica wagged her finger indignantly at her sister. "Why do you automatically assume that *I* did anything wrong? I did everything they asked me to do."

Matt leaned against the car, next to where Jessica was. "What did they ask you to do?"

A slow, bright smile spread across Jessica's face, rekindling the glow in her eyes. "They asked me to do a walk-on part in the movie."

Elizabeth stopped rocking back and forth. Her angry grimace melted into a look of delight. "Jess, that's great!"

Waves of excitement radiated off Jessica, scattering all over Matt like dappled sunlight. "I got a speaking part," she said.

"I can't believe it." Elizabeth grabbed Jessica's arm. "That's so awesome. What was your role?"

"It was a small but crucial part," she said coolly.

Matt pressed his lips together to hide his amusement. Jessica definitely knew how to play to her audience. Now that she had their full attention, she was composed and indifferent, tucking her enthusiasm away until she needed to spark their interest again.

Jessica folded her arms importantly across her chest. "I was in the most important scene in the movie. It was with Candice and Mason Avery Thomas."

Elizabeth's brow wrinkled. "I *love* him," she cooed. "He's a great actor."

"Mason plays a guy named Edgar, who'd just proposed to Julie, who is played by Candice. They're in this Italian restaurant, and Edgar pops the question. But see, there's this big moment, when the audience is dying to know what Julie's answer is, because she's fallen in love with her aerobics instructor." Jessica stopped to take a deep breath. "And that's where I come in."

"Let me guess," Matt said teasingly. "You play Edgar's ex-girlfriend, who wants to get back together with him."

Jessica shook her head. "I'm the waitress."

"The waitress," Elizabeth said thoughtfully. "What was your line?"

A new rush of enthusiasm swept over Jessica. "See, what happens is . . . I had to come in the second after Edgar proposes. The timing is very crucial. If it's not done right, it could spoil the entire mood," she said with drama. "I couldn't linger too long, or the moment would be lost. At the same time, I had to be fluid and graceful—not rushed."

"But what was your line?" Matt asked, sticking to the point.

Jessica pulled back her shoulders and lifted her head high, as though she were performing on stage. "I came in, holding a bottle of wine and two glasses. I uncorked the wine, poured a bit for Mason to try. He took a sip, and then I said"— Jessica paused for effect—*"Is it satisfactory, sir?"*

Elizabeth was quiet for a moment. "That's a good line," she said in an optimistic tone.

"I know it doesn't sound like much, but there's so much more to acting than meets the eye." Jessica gave her hair a confident toss. "You can't just show up and say the line. You have to *absorb* the character. You have to *become* the character," she said emphatically. "Matt can vouch for that. Acting is an art."

"She's absolutely right," he said, trying to keep a straight face. Jessica's passion reminded Matt of when he'd first started his own acting career, when he truly believed in the art. Initially, he'd been drawn in by the glamour of it all. But a few years down the road, he became disillusioned by the game playing, the Hollywood egos, the media. After a while, moviemaking wasn't glamorous anymore. It was just another job.

"So, I've made a decision," Jessica announced proudly. "I'm definitely becoming an actress!"

"That's nothing new." Elizabeth laughed. "You've wanted to become an actress since you were six."

Jessica smiled at Matt. "But this time I really mean it."

Matt looked down at his shiny leather boots. "If everything went so well, why did you get kicked off the set?"

"Right after I said my line, Candice got mad at me," Jessica answered. "At first, I thought it was because I'd done something wrong, but it turned out that she thought I was too pretty. Mason said she's totally insecure about her looks."

Matt rubbed his clean-shaven chin. "That sounds like Candice. She's a real dragon lady."

"So they're not going to use you in the film?" Elizabeth asked.

Jessica's face fell. "I guess not."

"I'm sorry, Jess." Elizabeth gave Jessica a sympathetic hug.

Matt touched her arm consolingly. "There'll be other chances, I promise."

"I hope so," she said.

Elizabeth's eyes clouded. "But we still have a serious problem, guys. Candice could be in danger. We have to warn her somehow."

"Why would I want to help her?" Jessica whined. "She cost me the biggest break of my life."

"This is serious, Jess," Elizabeth said. "It's not the time to be holding grudges."

A lock of hair fell across Matt's eyes. "Listen, why don't we hold off on warning Candice until I talk to Gomez at the waterfront tonight? He should give us some more details about the situation,"

Matt said in a low voice. "I'd hate to warn Candice and then find out we were wrong. She'd probably sue us or something."

"When do we have to be down by the water-front?" Elizabeth asked.

Matt pushed the hair out of his eyes. "At nine. But I'm going alone."

Jessica gripped his arm. "No way," she said adamantly. "We're going with you."

"It's too dangerous," Matt insisted. "I'm not going to risk having either of you hurt."

"Forget it. We won't let you go alone," Elizabeth said.

Matt sighed. He'd never encountered two more determined girls in his life. "Okay then, but we'd better get a move on," he said wearily. "If we don't get there in time, I'm afraid Gomez might have second thoughts."

"Are you sure this is the right bridge?" Jessica got out of the car, looking up at the dim lights of the bridge above. The soft, lapping sound of water seemed to be coming from a few yards away, but Jessica couldn't see. It was pitch-dark below.

"This has to be it," Matt said, shutting off the headlights. "I followed Gomez's instructions exactly."

Elizabeth crawled out of the tiny backseat and stretched her legs. "You get the back on the way home," she said firmly to Jessica.

Jessica stuck her tongue out in the dark. *Go*

*ahead, spoil my fun,* she thought to herself. It was a two-hour ride from the hotel to the bridge, but time seemed to fly by. With Matt in the driver's seat and Jessica sitting beside him, everything was ideal. They talked about acting, travel, parties—he'd even asked her about life at SVU. In the green glow of the dashboard, Jessica had stolen glances at his perfect profile and the way his gorgeous hair would sometimes swing across his cheek. Occasionally, when Matt reached for the stick shift, his fingers grazed Jessica's knee. The memory of it made her whole body tremble. It was as if they were living in a movie. *We're desperately in love and misunderstood by everyone,* Jessica fantasized. *It's me and Matt against the world.*

But then Elizabeth opened her mouth and spoiled the whole illusion.

"Is he here yet?" Elizabeth whispered in the darkness.

Jessica heard the crunch of Matt's boots in the gravel as he came around to the other side of the car. "I don't think so," she said. "But he could be down a little farther."

Elizabeth stood next to Jessica. "Should we stay here, or check things out?"

A prickly sensation tickled the back of Jessica's neck. The place was giving her the creeps. "Whatever you want to do," she said in a deep, steady voice.

Matt gently took her hand. The fear that had washed over her suddenly subsided. "Why don't we go and check it out?" he said.

"Okay," Jessica answered. She reached for her sister's hand, and they slowly made their way toward the water.

*Oh, if only Lila and Isabella could be here right now!* It wasn't fair. The only good thing to come out of this whole ordeal was that Jessica was able to meet Matt Barron, and Izzy and Li couldn't even see it for themselves.

Matt's fingers curled tenderly around Jessica's hand. His skin was warm and dry, and Jessica began to feel self-conscious about the cold dampness of her palms. She wanted to be brave for Matt, but her clammy hands gave it all away.

"Where's he supposed to be?" Jessica asked him.

"I'm not sure," Matt said. Jessica thought she detected a note of apprehension in his voice. "There's supposed to be a pay phone up ahead. If we can find that, he's supposed to be somewhere close by."

The lapping water grew louder as they trudged nearer to the river's edge. A dank, acrid smell tainted the air. Jessica took smaller footsteps. Wherever she turned, there was only blackness. The darkness seemed to be closing in on them.

Matt squeezed her hand gently. "We're almost there."

"I think I see the phone," Elizabeth said. "Look to the left."

Jessica saw it, too. There was the slightest glint

of metal a few feet ahead, reflecting the lights of the bridge. They'd found it.

"Gomez?" Matt whispered into the black night. "Gomez, are you there?"

Silence.

"Gomez?"

Jessica only heard the shallow sound of her breathing and the gritty sound of Elizabeth's sneakers on the gravel. Either no one was around, or someone was lurking, waiting for the perfect moment to strike.

"Ow!" Matt shouted.

"Are you okay?" Jessica asked worriedly.

"I'm fine," Matt said painfully. "My foot just found a bench for us to sit on."

Jessica waited for Matt to lead her to the bench; then she guided Elizabeth to it.

"He should be here by now," Elizabeth whispered. "I wonder if this is some kind of setup."

Jessica slid down the bench until the side of her leg pressed against Matt's. "I hope he gets here soon," she said. "This place is really weirding me out."

Even though they were sitting down, Matt still held firmly to Jessica's hand, as though he were afraid to let go. "We should wait a few minutes. He might show up soon."

"Maybe we should've gone to the police," Elizabeth said. There was a frightened edge to her voice that Jessica didn't hear very often. Elizabeth was rarely afraid of anything. If Elizabeth *was* scared of something, Jessica knew there had to be a good reason.

Jessica put her arm around her twin and pulled her close. "You know we couldn't have gone to the police. Remember the police chief and how he knew you were going to be in the Coffee House?"

Elizabeth rested her head against Jessica's shoulder. Her cheek was damp. "They can't all be involved."

"But how are we supposed to know who's involved and who isn't?" Jessica argued. "We can't trust anyone."

They sat quietly in the darkness, waiting for Gomez to arrive. A few cars drove across the bridge, their engines whirring past. There was an unspoken tension crackling in the air among them—a heavy feeling of impending doom. Gomez wasn't going to show up tonight, and they all knew it.

After a long period of silence, Matt finally spoke. "Let's go," he said in a thick voice. "It's too dangerous to stick around."

Jessica let Matt lead her back to the car, and Elizabeth followed behind her. Matt's fingers felt limp—weaker than they had just moments before. He was disappointed. Gomez was supposed to help unlock the mystery of Julia's death, and he hadn't delivered.

Jessica's heart ached for him. *Poor guy,* she thought as tears came to her eyes. *He's been through so much. If only this had worked out for him*. There was no doubt that the murder had a profound effect on Matt's life. Jessica couldn't help wondering if he'd ever be happy again.

Suddenly, something caught on Jessica's foot. It felt like a hat. She stepped forward to shake it off, when she bumped into a bigger object. It gave slightly, and Jessica tripped over it. A sharp, splintering scream escaped her throat. "There's a body!"

Matt caught Jessica in his strong arms. Jessica nuzzled her head against his chest for comfort. *What are you doing?* she thought with sudden embarrassment, pulling away. But Matt held her tightly, his arms encircling her. He needed her as much as she needed him.

"Where?" Elizabeth shrilled, backing away.

Jessica listened to the heavy thumping of Matt's heart. "Straight ahead."

Elizabeth pulled a penlight out of her purse. "I hope it's not Gomez," she said fearfully. Turning on the thin beam of light, Elizabeth moved in closer.

Jessica pressed her shaky palms flat against Matt's chest, wishing she could disappear into his arms and pretend all this wasn't happening. She turned toward the dim light and saw a ghostly pale man, with crimson blood trickling down the side of his head, his eyes wide open, looking up at the stars. Jessica looked away in horror.

"It looks like someone hit him over the head," Matt said quietly. A bloody metal pipe was laying near the victim's head.

Elizabeth closed the man's eyes. "I'm calling 911," she said.

"Don't go to the pay phone," Matt said as he reached into his pocket. "Use my cellular phone."

Elizabeth reached for the phone. Her sneakers crunched on the gravel as she moved a few feet away to make the call. Jessica still held on to Matt, his lean body pressed firmly against hers. Her mind was a ball of confusion, repulsed by the dead body at her feet, yet hopelessly attracted to Matt's powerful embrace.

"Do you think he was Gomez?" she whispered into his neck.

"Maybe we can find out," Matt said, pulling away from her. Jessica suddenly wished she could take the words back and Matt would go on holding her forever.

Jessica heard rustling sounds. "What are you doing?"

"Searching for some sort of ID," Matt answered.

Jessica stepped forward to help him look. The dead man's pockets were turning up empty.

"I don't think the guy even has a wallet," Matt said with frustration. "Maybe it was a robbery."

The pencil-thin beam of light shone in their direction, bringing Elizabeth along with it. "I called anonymously," she said. "We'd better hurry. The ambulance should be here any minute."

In the dull light, something glinted, catching Jessica's eyes. It was a pen in the man's shirt pocket. She examined it, noticing that something was engraved on the side of the pen. Jessica squinted and took a closer look. It read *G. B. Mammoth Pictures 1994*.

Stunned, Jessica tapped Matt numbly on the shoulder. "Guys," she said, holding the pen up to Elizabeth's light, "take a look at this."

"People involved with Mammoth are dropping like flies," Governor Dawson said. "Don't you think it's getting out of hand?"

Bishop switched the receiver from one ear to the other as he reached for his cigar box. Dawson sounded scared—and that was good. It put him exactly where Bishop wanted him. He let out a hearty laugh. "Since when have you taken such an interest in the movie business, Governor?"

"Since I started doing favors for *you*," he answered edgily. "When I told you I'd look the other way concerning Julia's death, I didn't think this sort of thing would be happening again."

Bishop clicked his tongue against the roof of his mouth. "You didn't do that as a favor for me—you did it for yourself," he said in a flat tone. "You're a smart man, Dawson. You know that if people start looking closely at the books and they see a few dollars missing here and there, they're going to know I took it." A menacing grin stretched across his fat lips. "And I won't hesitate to tell them where I spent it—at the track with my good friend George Dawson."

"Don't drag me into this, Ronald—"

"Oh, and the campaign contributions," Bishop interrupted. "I can't forget to mention those."

"I—I—I already helped you out," Dawson stammered. "What more do you want from me?"

"Your continued support."

"Ronald, we're talking about *murder*," Dawson said.

Bishop leaned back in his chair. "Who said anything about murder? We're talking about a suicide and an accident."

"It doesn't matter what you call it, I think we both know what's going on here." Dawson's voice hardened. "And I'm not about to condone it."

Bishop tilted his head back, blowing cigar smoke into the air above. It hung there in a bluish cloud over his head. "I didn't ask you to agree with my business methods. All I want is for you to keep your police officers out of my way."

"For heaven's sake, Bishop, think about what you're doing," Dawson pleaded. "If anyone finds out about my involvement—"

"It will be very unfortunate for you," Bishop finished unsympathetically. "And if you don't keep your mouth shut, you'll have a lot more to worry about than just your political career."

"I miss you so much," Tom said at the other end of the line.

Elizabeth twirled the telephone cord around her finger. "I miss you, too." The hotel drapes

194

were still closed, and she had no idea what the weather was like outside. "I hope I can see you soon. It's like being in prison."

"Too bad Gomez didn't get a chance to tell you anything," Tom said. "I feel so helpless having to stay away from you."

"I know, but it's for the best. Besides, I have Matt and Jessica to look after me," she said.

"And how are they doing?"

Elizabeth glanced around the room. It was amazing how empty it felt without them around. "They went out to pick up some breakfast," she said. "They seem to have hit it off surprisingly well. Jessica's completely starstruck, hanging on him every moment. But Matt doesn't really seem to mind."

"He must be a patient guy," Tom said.

Elizabeth nodded. "Matt's a great person."

"Nina says 'hi,'" Tom said. "I didn't give her any specifics, but I told her you were all right and that you'd try to be back as soon as you could."

"Poor Nina, I wish I didn't have to keep her in the dark." Elizabeth chewed her lip. "Were there any messages on my answering machine?"

Tom laughed. "Jessica got one from the entire SVU football team, calling to make sure she was okay."

Elizabeth rolled her eyes. "What else?"

There was a pause. "A man by the name of Alex Leary called. He says he's an FBI agent and that he wants to help you. It's probably a setup, just like everything else."

Elizabeth raised one eyebrow. "If he's for real, I wonder what he wants." She opened the drawer to the nightstand and took out a pen and piece of paper. "Where's he staying?"

"At the Hilton in Coral Cove. It's about halfway between L.A. and SVU," Tom said.

Elizabeth scribbled down the information. "Phone number?"

There was another pause. "I don't think you should call him," Tom finally said.

"I have to call him, Tom. What if he's the real deal? He might be our only way out."

"I realize that, but I know you. If I give you the number, you'll dash right over there without thinking twice," he said. "If you can sit tight for a few hours while I check the guy out, we can find out if it's safe for you to meet him."

"Honestly, Tom. Sometimes you act like I don't have a brain in my head."

"It's not that," Tom said. "But you have a tendency to dive into dangerous situations without taking precautions. All you have to do is wait a little while, then I'll call you and give you the number as soon as it's all clear. Okay?"

"Okay." Elizabeth's cheeks burned like those of a child who'd been scolded for crossing the street without looking both ways. "I'll talk to you later."

With the receiver still balanced on her shoulder, Elizabeth pressed her finger down on the hang-up button. She appreciated Tom's concern for her, but at times he got in the way. There was no way she was about to sit around and wait for him to check things out. She didn't have that kind of time.

Lifting her finger off the cradle, Elizabeth dialed the operator. "Yes . . . I need the number for the Hilton in Coral Cove."

# Chapter Twelve

"Agent Leary? This is Elizabeth Wakefield."

"I'm so glad you called," the man at the other end of the line said. His voice was serious and businesslike, but with a gentle undertone. "It was a wise decision."

Elizabeth exhaled audibly. There was something in the way he spoke that instantly put her at ease. This was someone who could be trusted. She could feel it in her gut. "What did you want to talk to me about?"

"Do you know a Detective Curtis?"

"Of course," Elizabeth replied. "He questioned me about the bombing."

"As you may know, Detective Curtis went on vacation," the agent continued. "But before he left, he contacted me about your case."

For days, hope had been dead inside her, but now it blossomed with expectation.

"I know all about your situation," Agent Leary said. "And I'm doing everything I can to get you and your sister out of it."

The heavy lead weight that had been sitting in the middle of Elizabeth's heart dissolved into a deluge of tears. "Thank you so much."

"For your safety, there's some important information I need to fill you in on—but for obvious reasons, I can't do it over the phone."

"I understand," Elizabeth said, wiping away her tears. "Should we meet?"

"That would be a good idea," the agent said. "There's a mall about five minutes from here, the Coral Reef Mall. We can meet there, on the lower level in front of the elevators."

Elizabeth wrote down the information.

"I'll be wearing a blue-and-green-striped shirt, a blue baseball cap, and sunglasses," he added. "I have dark hair and a mustache."

Elizabeth looked down at her clothes. "I'm wearing a white T-shirt and blue jeans. I have long blond hair—"

"That's all right, Elizabeth," he interrupted. "I already know what you look like. How long will it take you to get there?"

"About an hour," she said, studying the road map they'd taped to the wall.

The door to the hotel room opened. Jessica and Matt came in laughing, carrying bags of groceries.

Elizabeth waved, then turned her back to

them. "When should we meet?" she said quietly.

"Is noon all right?"

"Fine," she answered. "I'll meet you by the first-floor elevator at the Coral Reef Mall."

"Perfect," the agent said. "And make sure you drive carefully."

"I will." Elizabeth hung up the phone and casually smiled at her twin. "I'm starved," she said lightly. "What did you guys get?"

Jessica emptied the bag onto the table. "Doughnuts, muffins, a couple croissants, and some strawberries. They were Matt's idea."

Matt opened the second bag. "Don't forget the orange juice and bottled water."

"Sounds great." Elizabeth's stomach rumbled as she peered into the muffin box. She picked out a perfect cranberry orange muffin and licked the sugary glaze.

Jessica bit into a croissant. "Who was that on the phone?" she asked.

*Should I tell them?* Elizabeth wondered as she sank her teeth into the golden muffin. They had a right to know. After all, it involved them, too. Then again, they might have the same reaction as Tom, that the meeting was just a setup. Even though Elizabeth knew in her heart that it wasn't, she could have a tough time convincing Matt and Jessica. They'd hold her back. *I can't risk it,* Elizabeth decided. *This might be our only chance.*

Elizabeth worked steadily on her muffin, pretending she didn't hear the question.

*"Liz,"* Jessica said a little louder this time. "Who was that on the phone?"

Elizabeth put on her best poker face. "It was Tom," she said nonchalantly. "I'm meeting him later."

Pierce leaned quietly against the inside wall of the hotel closet. The sliding door was cracked a bit, and he could see the FBI agent clearly, sitting on the bed in his robe and talking on the phone.

The handle of a garment bag pressed uncomfortably against his back. Pierce stealthily reached into the pocket of his jacket and took out the silencer. The cool, smooth metal felt good in his hand as he screwed it onto the barrel of the gun. With one graceful motion, he loaded the clip. His hands were steady as he curled his fingers around the handle and trigger. He felt an all-consuming sense of power.

Pierce pressed his ear to the cracked door and listened. *The target is still on the phone.* That was his new name for people—*targets*. He'd been wrong to think of people as being made up of blood, bone, and flesh. It had been too painful to think of them in three dimensions, with family and friends—people who cared about them and would miss them. It was much easier to see them as paper bull's-eyes, flat and two-dimensional. *No one cries over a paper target.*

The FBI agent hung up the phone. His back was to the closet, and he started towel drying his hair. A little gremlin of guilt tugged at the corner of Pierce's heart, but he pushed it down fast, letting the coldness return. He wouldn't let himself feel anything anymore. The world didn't have room for emotions, it was just one big game. It was kill or be killed.

The target hung up the phone. Pierce slid back the door silently and rolled out on his side like an expert assassin. With rock-solid hands and outstretched arms, he aimed for the center of the target.

Two quick shots, and the target keeled over, falling to the floor. A big red spot in the middle of the white robe.

Bull's-eye.

Pierce walked around the body, over to the nightstand, and looked down at the slip of paper by the telephone. *E. Wakefield, Coral Reef Mall at noon. Lower level by elevators.* Even his uniform was carefully picked out: blue-and-green-striped shirt, blue baseball cap, sunglasses—all waiting for him on the chair. Luckily, Pierce already had dark hair and a mustache.

"I still have two hours until then," Pierce said. He pulled back the bloodstained bedcovers and tossed them onto the floor. Then he leaned back and turned on the television, flipping from one channel to the next. He'd sit and relax for a little while.

Then he'd go meet his next target.

\* \* \*

"Why did I give her the agent's name?" Tom complained out loud to himself as he drove furiously through the winding streets of Coral Cove.

It had been a careless move to tell Elizabeth anything at all. Elizabeth was an investigative reporter, and any reporter worth a nickel could've easily contacted Agent Leary based on the information Tom had given her. She'd said she would wait until he'd checked the situation out, but it was the slightest lilt in her voice that gave it all away. It said, *"Sure, Tom, I'll say whatever you want to hear, but as soon as I hang up this phone, I'm going to do exactly what I want."*

And that was why Tom had immediately jumped into his car and headed for Coral Cove at breakneck speed. He had to reach the hotel before Elizabeth did.

"Why won't you listen, Liz?" Tom said to his dashboard. Her stubbornness and independence often drove Tom to the brink of insanity, making him crazy with worry. But at the same time, it was that same spirit that had made him fall in love with her.

Tom turned into the Hilton parking lot. All the spaces at the front of the building were taken, so he swung around to the back. He didn't see Elizabeth's rented car. That was a good sign. *Or maybe it isn't.*

He parked in a spot next to the back entrance and cut the engine before the car came to a complete stop. Throwing the shift into park, Tom halted the car abruptly and jumped out, not bothering to lock the door. He raced to the back entrance.

It was locked.

Peering through the narrow window, he saw an elderly couple walking down the hallway.

*Please go out this way,* Tom silently begged. His stomach twisted itself into a tight ball of anxiety. What if Elizabeth needed help? There was no way he could reach her.

The elderly man opened the door, but Tom's stomach clenched itself even tighter. Tom held the door open as the couple stepped outside, trying to look as normal and unsuspecting as possible.

"Good morning!" Tom said with forced cheerfulness.

The man smiled at Tom. "Forget your key, did you?"

Tom nodded. "Thanks for letting me in. You have a good day now."

"Same to you," the elderly woman said.

As soon as the entrance was clear, Tom slipped into the building and walked down the hall, toward the elevator. He pressed the up button several times, but the elevator was already heading up. It would probably take five minutes for it to come back down again.

Tom dashed for the stairs.

He took them two at a time, up to the fourth floor, through the door, and then ran down the long, carpeted hallway. *Room 404 . . . 406 . . . 408 . . .*

Room 424 had to be at the other end. Tom raced ahead, dodging cleaning carts and people. He stayed close to the wall and turned the corner at full speed. Then . . . *bam!*

Tom ran headlong into a man wearing a blue-and-green-striped shirt, knocking him to the floor.

"I'm so sorry," Tom apologized, out of breath. He extended his hand to help the guy to his feet. "I didn't see you."

"If you'd been looking, you would've seen me," he snapped. Tom imagined that behind his sunglasses, the man's eyes were angry. The man touched all of his pockets as though he were afraid of losing something. "You better watch where you're going," the man seethed.

Tom picked up the blue baseball cap that had been knocked off the man's head and handed it to him. "Like I said, I'm sorry. I'm in a bit of a hurry."

"You're not the only one who's in a hurry," the man snarled, and snatched up the hat. Without another word, he continued down the hallway.

*What a grouch,* Tom thought to himself. He jogged down the hallway, thinking about all the precious time he'd wasted trying to apologize to that creep.

When Tom arrived at room 424, the door was slightly open. He knocked, but there was no answer. He knocked again. Still no answer. Carefully, Tom pushed the door open and walked inside.

The room was a mess, but no one was in sight. Towels were strewn everywhere, paper wrappers covered the floor. A garment bag and a small suitcase were open, the contents spilling out of the closet. Bedcovers were balled up on the floor. The television was blaring one of the local talk shows.

An eerie feeling trickled down like a fine mist, and Tom started to shudder. He closed the door behind him and slowly walked toward the bed. That's when he saw the deep red stain of blood soaking into the carpet. From under the bedcovers on the floor, Tom caught a glimpse of a man's foot.

*Oh no! They got to him, too.* Tom's teeth began to chatter. Had Elizabeth been here when it happened? He felt his stomach lurch with nausea. Moving over to the nightstand, Tom lifted the receiver and dialed the number for security.

"There's been an accident in room 424" was all he said before putting the receiver back on the hook. Out of the corner of his eye, he spotted a piece of paper with Elizabeth's name on it. It looked like an appointment. They were going to meet at the mall.

Tom ducked out of the room and ran, running faster than he ever had in his life.

# Chapter
# Thirteen

"Your package has arrived," the woman at the front desk announced over the phone. "I'll have the bellhop bring it up to you."

"That would be great, thanks." Matt hung up the phone and smiled at Jessica. "It's here!"

Jessica strolled over to the window and pulled back the drapes. "I feel like we're living in a cave," she said glumly.

Matt squinted in the intense sunlight. He held up his hand to shield his face. "You'd better keep those closed, Jess. Someone might be looking in."

Jessica sighed and closed them again. There was a knock at the door. Matt looked through the peephole, then opened the door, and took the package from the bellhop.

"Thanks a lot," Matt said, tipping him a twenty. The bellhop bowed slightly and closed the door on his way out.

"You're a generous tipper," Jessica said, plopping down on the unmade bed. "I think that's nice."

Matt sat down next to Jessica. "I've got to do something with all my extra money—might as well give it to other people."

Looking down at the package, Matt noticed the date stamped across the brown paper wrapper. He'd tried not to think about it, hoping the day would slip by without him even realizing it. But there it was, staring at him in bold, hateful numbers.

Today was supposed to be their wedding day.

Matt became unglued, as though the slightest movement would shatter him into a million fragments he'd never be able to put back together again.

"Are you all right?" Jessica's eyes were wide. "You're trembling!"

She looked down at the package, and without a word, she understood. Jessica put her arms around him, and Matt breathed in the sweet smell of her soft hair. He inhaled deeply, hoping the scent would fill the black chasm in his chest.

"I'm so sorry, Matt," she whispered. "You don't deserve any of this."

The tears started to fall, and he couldn't make them stop. It came from so far down inside, pulling up all the feelings he'd tried to ignore. Pain and loss roiled in the core of his heart, then bubbled unexpectedly to the surface. Every tear re-

208

lived that horrible day. Every tear was for Julia.

"I'm sorry," he sobbed.

"It's all right," Jessica said, rocking him gently. "Let it all out."

Matt dried his swollen eyes with the sleeve of his shirt. "This was supposed to be our—" His voice broke. "I never even had a chance to see her in the wedding dress. . . ."

Jessica's eyes were glistening with tears. "You two were meant to be together, I just know it," she said. "But some monster had to take it all away from you. We have to find out who did it, Matt." She held up the shiny gold pen they'd found in Gomez's pocket. "And it starts with this."

Matt pushed the package aside. "I'm not so sure I care anymore," he said. "Finding out who did it isn't going to bring her back."

Jessica held Matt's hands. "We can't give up now. Don't let them get away with it." She looked deeply into his eyes. "We have to do this for Julia."

Matt squeezed her tightly, knowing she was right. As hard as it might be, he had to push on. They had to find the killer.

He tore the brown wrapper off the package his agent had sent and set the book down on the bed. "If this can't help us, I don't know if anything can."

Jessica looked at the cover and read the title out loud. "*The Mammoth Pictures Executive*

*Directory*." She flipped through the book, which was about the same size as the Sweet Valley yellow pages. "Do you think we'll find Gomez's initials in here? What makes you so sure he's an executive?"

Matt rubbed his sore eyes. "They don't give gold pens to the camera crew. It's definitely the sort of thing you'd find only in the top-level offices," Matt said. "They like their executives to be a bit showy."

"We'll start at the very top and work our way down," Jessica said, running her finger down the list.

Matt put his head on the pillow and closed his eyes. A feeling of calm hit him. He couldn't fall apart, he had to be strong to see this tragedy to the end. Alone, Matt didn't think he'd be able to do it; but with Jessica nearby, anything seemed possible.

A moment later, Matt felt a light tapping on his foot. "I found three matches so far," Jessica said softly. "Maybe we should try them out."

Matt picked up the phone. "Who's the first one?"

"Gordon Beal," she answered, then read his home phone number to Matt. "He's the Assistant Vice President of Marketing and Research."

The line was ringing. After three rings, a man picked up the phone. "Hello?"

Matt cleared his throat. "Is this Gordon Beal?"

"Yes, and to whom am I speaking?"

*Click.* Matt hung up the phone. "I didn't have

time to chat," he said dryly. "That one's alive and well."

"Okay, let's try Gary Bellamy—he's in Script Acquisitions."

Matt punched in the number. A woman answered. "May I please speak with Mr. Bellamy?"

"I'm sorry, he's not in right now. May I take a message?" she said.

"No, thank you. I'll try back later." Matt hung up. "That one's a bust."

Jessica returned to the book. "At least we're narrowing it down. Try Gilbert Bradley. He's the Assistant to the Executive Vice President, Richard McKenna."

Matt dialed the number.

"Hello?" It was a woman.

"I'd like to speak with Gilbert Bradley, please."

The other end of the line went silent. "Who are you?" the woman asked. Her voice was thick, as though she'd been crying.

Matt signaled Jessica. She moved in closer. "I'm an old friend. We went to high school together. I happened to be in the area and . . . I wanted to see how Gill was doing."

The woman broke down. "You can't speak with him," she cried, "He was murdered last night."

*Bingo!* Matt mouthed to Jessica. She circled the name in the book.

"Oh no. What a terrible shock. I'm so sorry, ma'am." Even though Matt didn't know Gilbert Bradley, his sympathy was real. He knew the pain

211

she was going through. A tear ran down his cheek. "Do you know who did it?"

"It was a robbery," she said through her tears. "They dumped his body by the waterfront. Gilbert would never go there."

A tear ran down Matt's face. "I don't know what to say—"

"There's nothing to say," she answered. Then the line went dead.

The phone dropped from Matt's hands. He looked at Jessica, his golden eyes swollen from tears. "When is it going to end, Jess?" he said desperately. "When is the killing going to end?"

"Hi, Elizabeth. I'm Mr. Leary," said the man with the sunglasses and baseball cap. "I'm glad you could make it."

Elizabeth nodded nervously at the FBI agent, watching him press the button for the mall elevator. An awkward silence fell between them, one that she was anxious to fill. "I hope I'm not late. I got lost."

"No," Agent Leary said. "You're not late at all."

The doors to the glass elevator car opened, and a crowd of shoppers spilled out until the entire car was empty. Leary motioned for Elizabeth to step inside. They were alone.

"Listen carefully and follow my instructions," he said coldly. His tone was flat and metallic, lacking the warmth Elizabeth had heard over the phone. "When the doors open, we'll walk casually to the portion of the mall that's under construction. Take hold of my left arm and stay on that side always. Keep your eyes focused straight ahead. People might be watching. This is for your own safety."

Elizabeth ran through the checklist in her mind. The elevator car stopped, and the doors opened.

"Are you ready?" he asked.

"Yes," Elizabeth said. She took his left arm and they strolled casually out of the elevator.

"Very good," he said in a monotone. "Keep going, just like this. When we're at a safe distance, I'll fill you in on everything."

Elizabeth swallowed hard. Something was wrong, but she couldn't put her finger on it. It was a vibe she was picking up. *I should've brought Jess and Matt along with me,* she thought to herself. They passed a busy toy shop, packed with children. Part of her was tempted to break free and run into the store, to hide somewhere in the cluttered aisles. *Get real, Liz,* a voice of reason whispered to her. *You can't hide from an FBI agent.*

She held on to his arm as they continued on, past a jewelry store, a pretzel stand, and four boutiques. Leary looked from side to side as they walked, not saying a thing. He seemed paranoid, as if someone were going to jump out at them at any minute. It was as if some invisible danger were swarming around them. Elizabeth was scared. She decided it was good that she didn't tell Jess, after

213

all. *I got her into this mess all by myself,* Elizabeth thought. *It's up to me to get her out.*

Pierce's finger was poised on the trigger. Underneath his jacket, his arm rested against his stomach, the barrel aimed directly at Elizabeth's side. As soon as they reached a secluded area, it was time for target practice.

"We're almost there," he said, looking ahead at the draped plastic of the construction site.

Elizabeth didn't say anything. She was a good target. She did exactly as she was told and didn't talk about herself. He hated it when targets started rambling on about themselves. They started showing their dimensions. It was better when he didn't know anything. Then they were just pieces of cardboard.

"Is someone after us right now?" Elizabeth blurted out all of a sudden.

Pierce was startled. "Yes."

"Where are they? I don't see anyone," she said.

Pierce's temper started to flare. She was talking. He didn't want to hear her voice. "They're everywhere. Don't talk right now, it's too dangerous."

Elizabeth fell silent. Her grip on his arm tightened. Pierce pushed the gun closer to her side. Sweat beaded his mustache.

A barricade had been set up to keep shoppers from crossing into the construction zone. The sight was abandoned because it was a weekend, but Pierce took a quick look around, just in case. He moved one of the wooden sawhorses that was blocking the entrance and walked through, with Elizabeth in tow.

"Is it safe to be in here?" Elizabeth said nervously.

"Shh." Pierce looked up into the exposed rafters. Bishop's men must've had the place surrounded, but there was no sign of them anywhere. They were hiding, waiting, and the second Pierce missed his shot at Elizabeth, they'd take aim at him.

But that didn't matter. He wouldn't dare miss this time.

Elizabeth's fingers trembled against his arm. Her blue-green eyes were filled with what looked like terror and fear of the unknown. "Is it safe?" she asked again.

Sweat trickled down the side of Pierce's face. "You have to trust me, Elizabeth," he said heavily. The gun inched closer to her side. "I'm going to take care of you."

*I can't go any farther.* Tom gasped for air and grabbed the railing that circled the second floor of the mall. A stabbing pain wrenched his side. If he took another step forward, he was afraid he might collapse.

"I've been through this mall four times. Where are they?" Tom wondered aloud. The more he thought about it, the more likely it seemed that

215

whoever was meeting Elizabeth would have taken her far away by now. Tom's spine was frozen in terror. If that was the case, he may never be able to find her.

The construction area loomed ahead. *Would he take her there?* With every trip through the mall, he'd avoided the site. But now, on this fourth time, something seemed terribly wrong about it. There was something suspicious about the whole area. Then he suddenly realized what it was.

The barricade had been moved.

Without a second's hesitation, Tom ran to the construction area, adrenaline pulsing through his veins. His lungs struggled for air, but Tom pushed harder, sprinting toward the wooden sawhorses, using every ounce of energy his body had left. With a powerful kick, he lifted his leg high in the air and sailed over the barricade.

Off to the left, in an empty storefront, Tom caught a glimpse of a man in dark glasses and a blue baseball cap. Elizabeth was holding his arm, her posture slumped in fear. A bolt of anger shot through him with a grim realization: *He's the guy I bumped into at the hotel.*

A rallying cry escaped Tom's lips as he jumped through the air and landed on the man's back. "Leave her alone!" he screamed as they both fell.

The man's gun slid across the floor.

Elizabeth jumped away. "Tom, what are you doing?"

Tom wrapped his arms in a bear hug around

the man, pinning his arms to his sides. "What were you going to do to her?" Tom shouted into his ear.

"Tom, he's an FBI agent!" Elizabeth cried out. "Let him go!"

The man twisted from side to side, scrambling to get loose. "You'd better let go of me, or you could land yourself a few years in prison," the man hissed.

"Tom, let him go!" Elizabeth said. "He wants to help us!"

Tom flipped the man on his back and tied his wrists together with a length of electrical wire. "He's no FBI agent," Tom panted. "The real agent is back at the Hilton with a bullet hole through his chest."

Elizabeth clasped her hand over her mouth. "Oh no!"

"Quick, Liz, get security!" Tom said, holding the man down with his knee. In a fit of rage, Tom ripped off the man's hat and sunglasses and threw them against the wall.

"Let me remind you that it's a federal offense to assault an FBI agent," the man said.

"Save it, you loser," Tom snapped. "Where are your friends? Are they hiding out nearby?"

"I don't know what you're talking about."

Tom looked up to see if security had arrived yet. A second later, a blinding flash cracked against the side of his head, as the man swung his tied fists, sending Tom reeling backward and onto the floor. Hot pain seared his temple. He lay there in agony, listening to the hurried footsteps of the man as he made his escape toward the exit doors.

Tom slowly lifted his head, then everything went black.

# Chapter
# Fourteen

"Are you sure we're doing the right thing?" Jessica asked, looking at the modest white house and neat green lawn in front of it. "I mean, her husband just died."

Matt parked the Ferrari on the street and turned on the security system. "We don't have much choice. Other people could be in danger."

Hand in hand, they walked up the paved driveway to the front door. Jessica gripped Gilbert Bradley's gold pen in one hand and braced herself for the worst.

Matt rang the doorbell. "Don't worry about a thing," he said reassuringly. "I'll do all the talking."

The door opened slowly, and a woman appeared in the doorway, staying behind the screen door. *She's so young,* Jessica thought. *Too young to be a widow.* She couldn't have been more than thirty years old. Sadness creased the woman's face and dulled her eyes. Deep sympathy stirred inside Jessica; if she could've given Mrs. Bradley a piece of her own happiness, she would have.

Matt took off his sunglasses. "I know this is a bad time, Mrs. Bradley, but I need to ask you a few questions."

"Who are you?" she asked.

"I'm Matt, and this is Jessica," he said, gesturing toward her. "We have reason to believe that your husband's death wasn't a robbery, but that someone was out to get him."

Mrs. Bradley looked at Matt, then at Jessica. Her eyes darted suspiciously from one to the other.

"We have something that belongs to you," Jessica said. She extended her hand and pressed the gold pen against the screen. "I feel so badly about what happened to your husband."

The woman opened the screen door and hesitantly took the pen. She covered her trembling mouth with her fingertips. "Where did you get this?"

"We found it," Matt said vaguely. "We're not here to bother you, only to find out if you have any information about Gilbert's death."

"We think other people might be in danger," Jessica added. "We really need your help."

Mrs. Bradley held the pen against her protectively. "Look, I don't know who you are. Why should I believe what you're saying?" Her voice was rough-edged, like a chipped drinking glass. Jessica had the feeling that she might break apart at any moment. "As far as I'm concerned, this is harassment," she said.

"Believe me, we don't mean to cause you any more distress," Matt said. "But we need to know if anything unusual happened before your husband died. Was there anyone new he was in contact with? Was he acting differently?"

Mrs. Bradley's eyes narrowed with suspicion. She crossed her arms and stared at them without saying a word.

Jessica pressed her hand against the screen. "I know you don't think you can trust anyone right now—we're feeling the same way. We want to stop these people before they hurt anyone else," she said. "We think Candice Johannsen might be the next victim."

The woman's features softened slightly. Her mouth opened as if she were about to speak, when suddenly she closed it again and took a step backward. She slammed the door shut.

Jessica banged on the door with her fist. "Please, Mrs. Bradley . . . other people's lives are in danger!"

Matt took Jessica by the wrists and pulled her away from the door. "Don't, Jess. You'll scare her even more." He stepped closer to the door and shouted so that Mrs. Bradley could hear. "Thank you for your time. I'm leaving a number where we can be reached if you change your mind." Matt wedged a slip of paper into the crack of the screen door.

"Now what?" Jessica said dejectedly.

Matt squeezed her hand. "All we can do is wait, and hope she comes around."

Ronald Bishop crushed the stub of his cigar into a silver ashtray and loosened his red silk necktie. Angry purple veins bulged along the sides of his neck. "I can't believe you missed her twice."

Pierce swung his legs up, stretching out on the leather couch. He tilted his head back and stared at the ceiling with bored detachment.

"I gave my men orders to kill you if you missed again," Bishop continued as he paced the plush office. "But they were laughing so hard when they saw you get tackled by a college boy that they forgot to shoot."

Pierce rubbed his sore wrists. They still stung from the wire that stupid kid had tied him up with. "There weren't any backup men," he answered calmly.

Bishop stopped dead in his tracks. "What did you just say?"

"I *said*, the whole story about backup men with orders to shoot is one big lie." Pierce laced his fingers behind his head. "Just like all the other lies you've told."

Bishop extracted the red silk handkerchief from his breast pocket and dabbed at his forehead.

"Why would I lie about something like that?"

Pierce's sinister laughter filled the office. "Really, Ronald, think about how ridiculous your story is," he said, still looking up at the ceiling. "There I was, being beaten up by this kid while Elizabeth is standing somewhere off in the corner. Now, you're telling me that you had fifty men hiding, waiting for me to mess up so they could bump me off." He turned and glowered at Bishop. "If you're so bent on seeing Elizabeth Wakefield dead, any one of those guys could've easily killed her."

"It was your job to finish," Bishop countered.

"It was my job because you couldn't find anyone else," Pierce said flatly. "I was the only one stupid enough to do it."

Bishop walked over to the couch and towered above Pierce. "So what are you saying? Are you leaving me hanging with this whole deal? Are you just going to walk away?" His steel gray eyes held Pierce's stony gaze. "There are two more jobs to be done."

"I've given it some thought, and I've come to the conclusion that it would be foolish to leave at this point in the game."

Bishop chuckled. "You know I have far too much on you to let you leave." He nodded toward his desk. "All I have to do is pick up that phone, and you'll be on your way to prison."

Pierce rubbed his hands together with delight. "See, this is where it starts getting fun," he said, sitting up. "I'm no longer your subordinate. We're equals. I have just as much on you."

"You have nothing on me," Bishop scoffed.

"Conspiracy, gambling, extortion, accessory to murder—four counts." Pierce gave Bishop a brotherly slap on the back. "Looks like we're partners, buddy!" He sighed loudly. "I've waited so long for this day."

Bishop's thick lips curved in an uncertain smile. "So you're going to finish the job?"

"Absolutely," Pierce answered. "And then, when this whole thing is over, you're going to give me half of all the money you've helped yourself to."

"I can't do that—"

"You can . . . and you *will*," Pierce corrected.

Bishop's head lowered a fraction. "I suppose we could work something out." He wiped his damp brow. "In the meantime, what about the Wakefield girl?"

Pierce toyed with the ends of his mustache. "It'll be tough to get at her now that she's got that little entourage with her." His eyes became narrow slits. "The only solution is to build another bomb, and wipe them all out at once."

Ronald Bishop paused for a moment, then nodded slowly. "I like the way you think."

"I can't believe you'd do something so stupid!" Jessica threw her hands up in disbelief. "How could you agree to meet some stranger

224

without telling us? Are you completely insane?"

"That was yesterday, Jess. You've been harping on me since last night. Can we just forget about it?" Elizabeth stood behind Tom, examining the bandages on his head. "How do you feel?" she asked him.

"It hurts a little," Tom said meekly.

Elizabeth pouted. "Where?"

Tom pointed to the side of his head. "Here . . ."

Tilting his head gently to the side, Elizabeth kissed him directly on the spot. "Anywhere else?"

Tom nodded. "Right here . . . ," he said, pointing to his forehead.

Elizabeth kissed him there, too. "Where else?"

Jessica stood up angrily. "Would you two stop it? This lovebird routine is making me nauseous!" She turned to Matt, who was watching the morning news on TV. "Would you talk some sense into her?"

Matt flipped from station to station without looking up from the TV. "Jess, I'm sure your sister realizes she made a mistake. Elizabeth's learned her lesson."

"Thank you, Matt," Elizabeth said.

Jessica pounced on the bed Matt was sitting on. "Whose side are you on, anyway?"

Tom touched his head and groaned. "Jess, would you knock it off? Enough already. Liz isn't going to do it again."

"This is just great!" Jessica stomped around the room. "Now everyone's against me! Go ahead,

side with good old Liz. But in case you've all forgotten, she's the reason why we're stuck in this
room like a bunch of circus animals!"

Matt turned the volume up a notch.

Elizabeth gritted her teeth. "I went by myself
yesterday because I felt guilty. I felt bad for getting you mixed up in this mess, and I wanted to
straighten it out by myself. Two seconds ago you
yelled at me for *not* dragging you along yesterday,
and now you're yelling at me for getting you involved. Make up your mind!"

"Keep it down, guys." Tom stood between the
two of them. "We don't want hotel security coming up here."

Elizabeth moved around him. "Stay out of this,
Tom."

He looked insulted. "What did I do?"

"Nothing, that's the problem!" Jessica blurted
out. "You've spent half the time back at school, all
nice and safe while some maniac is after us."

"I was doing research!" Tom said defensively.

Matt turned the volume up again.

Jessica's blood was boiling. "Researching what?
How to go on with your normal routine when
your girlfriend's life is in danger?"

"Don't talk to him like that!" Elizabeth
shouted.

"Hey, shut up a minute!" Matt yelled, turning
up the volume.

Everyone stopped and looked at the TV. The
words *Special Report* were on the screen.

The announcer had a dour expression on her face as she stared into the camera. *"Topping the news this morning . . . leading Hollywood actress Candice Johannsen was found dead in her apartment early this morning. . . ."*

Jessica covered her face with her hands. They'd been right, Candice *was* the next one, but they couldn't manage to save her.

*"While the cause of death is still unknown, preliminary reports say that a drug overdose is a strong possibility. Ms. Johannsen had a history of drug abuse, but autopsy reports won't be able to confirm the cause of death for at least a week. . . ."*

Elizabeth sank to the floor. "I can't believe it."

*"Ms. Johannsen was currently working on a New Vision Studios film called* Forbidden Desire, *scheduled to be released this summer. No word yet if the studio plans to find a replacement to complete the film or scrap the project altogether."*

Matt clicked off the TV. The room was still as each of them collected their thoughts.

Jessica started to cry. "We knew all along. We could've done something."

Matt touched her hair. "We didn't have much to go on. We did the best we could with what we had."

"I feel terrible," Elizabeth said, holding Tom's hand. "We have to work fast before they hit again."

Matt shook his head. "But if we don't even know who's next, how can we stop them?"

The phone rang, and Jessica answered it. "Hello?"

"Is this Jessica?"

"Yes, who's this?"

"Mrs. Bradley," the voice said. "I saw the report this morning. It's horrible."

Jessica wiped a tear from her cheek. "We all feel badly."

"I'm sorry I drove you away yesterday," she apologized. "After you left, I came across something unusual. Something you might be interested in."

Jessica looked at Matt. "We'll be right over."

# Chapter Fifteen

"I was going through my husband's desk, and I found this." Mrs. Bradley handed Jessica a small red envelope with the words *Mammoth Pictures* printed in black ink. "Gilbert never told me he had a safe-deposit box."

Jessica took a seat at the Bradleys' kitchen table and opened the envelope. Inside were two gold keys. "What do you think is inside the box?"

"I have no idea, other than that it's probably work related," Mrs. Bradley said. She handed Matt a glass of iced tea. "From what you've told me, it sounds like it might be the sort of thing you're looking for."

Jessica and Matt exchanged looks. "Can I borrow your phone?" Jessica asked.

"Of course," Mrs. Bradley answered, pointing to the one on the wall by the door.

"I'm going to tell Liz to meet us at the bank," Jessica said to Matt.

Matt nodded, then took a sip of iced tea. He leaned forward with his elbows on the table, an earnest expression on his face. "Thank you for helping us. I can't tell you how much I appreciate it." A surge of emotion welled up inside him. "I feel bad about bothering you during such a difficult time. I went through the same thing myself about two weeks ago."

Mrs. Bradley reached across the table and touched Matt lightly on the back of the hand. "When you came by yesterday, I didn't make the connection. Then it dawned on me this morning. I'm so sorry about what happened to Julia."

Matt sighed. "I wish I could tell you that the pain goes away, but so far it hasn't. It's only been getting worse. Every time I think about her, it's like a knife twisting in my side."

"I feel like I'm walking through a fog, and everything seems unreal," Mrs. Bradley said. "People have been telling me, 'You're young, you'll get over it,' but I don't see it. I don't see any future at all."

Matt swallowed hard. He knew exactly what she was talking about. Ever since Julia had died, his life was broken down into tiny increments. At first, Matt could only look ahead as far as five minutes, trying to get through that block of time without losing his mind. Then it was half an hour, then an hour, and then when he'd realized she'd been murdered, he looked ahead to the time when her killer would be brought to justice. He still didn't know when that time would come, but it loomed ahead of him as sharp as the blade of a knife. Beyond that, there was nothing else.

"Liz and Tom are on their way over to the bank," Jessica said, hanging up the phone.

They walked to the front door.

"Is there anything we can do for you?" Matt turned and asked Mrs. Bradley.

She shook her head. "My family's taking good care of me."

Jessica's eyes looked troubled. "Do you have anywhere else you can stay? I'm worried that someone might come looking for the key if they know it's here."

"As soon as the funeral's over, I'm flying back East to stay with my parents for a while," she said softly. "I can't stand living in this house."

"Keep yourself safe until then," Matt said. "And don't tell anyone about seeing us."

"I won't," she promised.

Jessica smiled sympathetically. "Take care, and thank you."

Mrs. Bradley nodded, closing the door.

"Well, this is it," Jessica said, handing the little red envelope to Matt. "Let's keep our fingers crossed."

"Right this way," the bank officer said, leading Elizabeth down the long, narrow hallway to the gleaming metal vault. Inside, there were hundreds of numbered rectangular boxes, each with two keyholes.

"What number are we looking for?" the officer asked.

Elizabeth looked down at the red envelope. "Two, six, four, two," she read aloud.

"That would be over here," the officer said, pointing toward the back of the vault. She located the box, then inserted her master key into one of the keyholes. "Put your key in the other lock, and on the count of three, turn clockwise."

Elizabeth inserted the key.

"One, two, three . . ." The tiny rectangular door opened. Reaching in, the officer took out a long, slender metal box and set it down on the counter that ran along the outer wall. "I'll wait for you outside. Please take your time."

"Thanks," Elizabeth said. As soon as the officer left, she lifted the lid. Inside the box was a white business envelope. Elizabeth took the envelope, shoved it into her purse, and walked out of the vault.

"I'm all set, thank you," she called to the officer without stopping. She was dying to see what was in the envelope. It called to her, drew her toward it with the force of an electromagnet. But Elizabeth resisted, holding on until she reached the rest of the group.

"What does it say?" Jessica asked, opening the door to the rental car. "Did you open it?"

Elizabeth slipped into the backseat with Tom, taking the envelope out of her purse. "No, I waited for you guys."

"What willpower!" Jessica said, ripping the envelope from her sister's hands. .

"Take it easy, Jess," Tom said. "You wouldn't want to destroy any important evidence."

Matt leaned over Jessica's shoulder. "There are two letters," Jessica said.

Elizabeth and Tom leaned over the front seat. "Read it out loud," Elizabeth said.

"The first letter is from Gilbert Bradley," Jessica said, scanning the letter. "This is what it says:

*"To Whom It May Concern:*

*"If you get this letter, it means I'm already dead. I stumbled upon some information two days ago that's put me in a great deal of danger. I figured this letter was the only way to protect the information if they got to me, and as you can see, I was right.*

*"I started working for Mammoth Pictures five years ago as an assistant to Richard McKenna, the executive vice president. My time with Mammoth was fairly uneventful up until the day before yesterday. I was at McKenna's desk when I found a memo signed by Ronald Bishop, CEO of Mammoth Pictures. (I've enclosed the memo with this letter.) While it looks like a regular memo, you'll notice that the details are consistent with the murder of Julia Reynolds. Details are also given for two other actors, and I'm hoping you'll be able*

*to use this information to stop them in time.*

*"I should've gone to the authorities im-
mediately, but instead I held on to the memo
and waited. McKenna is acting strangely,
and I have a feeling he knows I have the
memo. That's why I've put it away for safe-
keeping.*

*"Good luck, and please tell my wife that I
love her.*

*Gilbert Bradley"*

A chill ran down Elizabeth's spine. Impulsively,
she snatched the envelope out of Jessica's hands
and studied the memo.

*Memo: Confidential
To: Richard McKenna, Executive VP
From: Ronald Bishop, CEO
Re: Former Mammoth Clients*

*As you are already aware, several important
Mammoth clients have recently signed over to
New Vision Studios. While the situation dis-
pleases us, we hold no grudge and would like to
give the actors an opportunity to come back to
us. Here's a schedule I've set up for meetings
with the actors. Since I will not be able to attend,
my assistant, Pierce, will be there on my behalf.*

*Julia Reynolds: March 1, on New Vision
set. Our stocks have fallen significantly since*

*Julia left. She had a history of depression during her time at Mammoth—she may need a little push to steer her in the right direction.*

*<u>Candice Johannsen</u>: March 15, at her home. A legendary woman of substance, Candice should be treated with great care. Bring her a bottle of wine and anything else she craves. Watch out, though, she does have a history of overdoing it.*

*<u>Philip Markham</u>: March 17, during the Academy Awards. Inside sources say that Philip is favored to win the Oscar for Best Supporting Actor this year. Our best shot would be to congratulate him right after he receives his award. It's still rumored that an obsessive fan has been stalking Philip; therefore, be prepared for tight security.*

"I can't believe they'd try to kill someone at the Academy Awards!" Jessica shouted. "How do you think they'll do it?"

Elizabeth reread the last paragraph. "It's nearly impossible for anyone to get onstage when an actor is accepting an award, so it has to be something they can do from a distance."

Matt looked at the memo. "Wait a minute," he said, pointing to the paper. "Right here it says 'our best shot'—they're going to shoot him onstage."

Tom buckled his seat belt. "It's a good thing

we found this memo when we did. We can take it to the police right now."

"No, we can't," Elizabeth said adamantly. "Bishop still has a lot of the police force in his back pocket."

Jessica frowned. "So what are we going to do?"

Matt started the car. "The only thing we *can* do," he said in a grave tone. "We'll have to stop them ourselves."

"This is where you live?" Jessica's jaw dropped as she walked through the door of the penthouse apartment. "This place is absolutely incredible."

"It really *is* nice," Elizabeth said, treading carefully on the black-and-white tile floor.

Tom trailed behind, admiring the black-lacquer and chrome furniture. "If you ever need someone to house-sit, let me know."

"Thanks," Matt said. He led the three of them into the dark living room, where the lighted aquarium coffee table glowed like a floating spaceship. A stack of unopened mail waited for him on the credenza. He picked up the pile and started flipping through. "The video camera is in the closet behind you," he said to Elizabeth. "It's kind of small. I hope it can do the job."

Elizabeth opened the closet door. "I'm sure it'll be fine."

"Let's set up over here, Liz," Tom said, plopping himself down on one of the oversized leather chairs.

Jessica leaned on the lighted aquarium tabletop with her elbows and stared into the shining blue depths. Matt looked up from his mail and watched as the shimmering light danced across Jessica's lovely features.

"It's beautiful, isn't it?" she said, pointing to the golden angelfish.

Matt nodded, his eyes fixed on her. "It is."

Jessica looked up, meeting his gaze. She bit her lip as a lock of hair fell softly against her cheek.

Suddenly the lights came on, and the mood evaporated.

Tom unplugged one of the chrome floor lamps and dragged it over to one of the leather chairs. "I hope you don't mind," he said. "We need as much light as possible."

"Go right ahead," Matt said, returning to his mail. There were the usual bills, junk mail, and written requests for interviews. A postcard from Bridget was mixed in, saying that everything was going well in New York. At the very bottom of the stack was a large envelope with no return address. It had been hand delivered.

"I have no idea what this one is," Matt said, holding it up to the light. The paper was thick and pulpy, with gold trim. He couldn't see what was inside.

"Open it and find out." Jessica slid across the couch to make room for Matt.

Tom finished setting up all the lights, arranging them in a half circle around the chair. Elizabeth popped a blank videotape into the camera and handed it to Tom. "Let's roll," she said.

"Do you know what you're going to say?" Tom asked, looking through the camera lens. "Maybe you should write it down."

"Nah," Elizabeth said, falling into the chair. "I'm just going to wing it."

Matt ran his finger under the gold seal. The envelope was unusually thick and bulky.

Jessica leaned toward him to get a closer look. "It's probably one of those magazine subscription contests. Their envelopes get more elaborate every time."

Matt pulled out the contents. It was another envelope. This one also had a gold seal, but the paper had a finer texture. "I wish they'd put a return address on here. That way I'd know if it was worth going through all the trouble."

"Okay, guys, quiet over there," Elizabeth said, sitting up in the chair. "We're starting to tape."

Tom focused the camera, then held up five fingers, counting backward down to one.

Elizabeth cleared her throat and leaned toward the camera. "Hello, my name is Elizabeth Wakefield, and I'm a student at Sweet Valley University. What I'm about to tell you is a completely true account of the illegal practices of Mammoth Pictures. . . ."

Matt broke the second seal. Inside was a white cardboard square with two flaps folded over each other. Gold swirls decorated the outside.

"My involvement began soon after a paper I wrote was finished, and my professor, Cynthia

Zartman, decided to send it off to the *Hollywood Daily* to be published. That day, Professor Zartman was killed by a mail bomb. . . ."

Jessica leaned closer. Gingerly, Matt opened the flaps.

"Oh, wow!" Jessica shouted.

Elizabeth stopped speaking, and Tom turned off the camera. "What is it?" she asked.

Jessica waved the cardboard in the air. "They're giving a special award in honor of Julia at the Oscars tomorrow! And they want Matt to accept it for her!"

"That's wonderful news," Elizabeth said.

A bittersweet mixture of pride and sadness caught in Matt's throat as he stared down at the white-and-gold invitation. Winning an Oscar was Julia's dream, and in the past several years, she'd worked so hard to achieve that goal. And now she had made it—but the honor came too late. Matt hoped that wherever Julia's spirit was, she'd know that her dream had come true.

Jessica waved a hand in front of Matt's face, breaking him from his trance. "You *are* going to accept the award, aren't you?" she asked.

"Of course," Matt said thickly. "I wouldn't miss it for anything." His body felt limp and ragged. "There's one problem, though."

Jessica's blue-green eyes clouded with concern. "What's that?" she asked.

"I don't have anyone to go with," Matt said. His melancholy fingers traced the gold lettering on the VIP passes. "Jessica, would you be my date for the Academy Awards?"

# Chapter Sixteen

"Everything's all set," Matt said to Elizabeth as he hung up the phone. "You've got the job."

Unable to contain herself, Jessica jumped up from the leather couch, waving her arms wildly in the air. "Did you hear that, Liz? You got the job!"

"I heard," Elizabeth answered, eyeing Jessica strangely. "It's good news. It's exactly what we needed."

Matt spread out a map of the Shrine Auditorium across the top of the aquarium. He made *X* marks on it with a black felt-tipped pen, as if he were planning a football strategy.

*"Needed?"* Jessica's voice reached a high pitch. "You're going to be escorting the Hollywood elite offstage after they've accepted their awards, in front of millions of people. I can't believe you're not even a little bit excited."

"I don't care about schmoozing with the rich

and famous," Elizabeth said, turning her attention to the floor plan of the auditorium where the awards ceremony was going to be held.

If they weren't identical twins, Jessica would've sworn at that very moment that her sister was adopted. How could she not care about meeting movie stars? "Do you hear what you're saying?" Jessica asked incredulously.

Elizabeth sighed. "Jess, these people are normal human beings, just like us. Acting is just another job. The only difference is they're constantly in the spotlight." Elizabeth smiled sheepishly in Matt's direction. "No offense."

"None taken, Liz. You're absolutely right," Matt said as he connected a few of the X's with arrows. "We're just like everyone else."

Jessica stared dreamily at Matt's smooth olive complexion and sensuous mouth. *He's so humble,* she thought as she felt her muscles dissolving into a jellylike substance. *And he's my date to the Academy Awards.* The very thought sent volts of electricity shooting through every molecule of her being.

"Let's go over the plan," Elizabeth said, pointing to the notes Matt had made.

His finger hovered above the X to the left of the stage. "You'll be here most of the time." His finger traced the arrow that led to the center of the stage. "Except for when you escort the actors offstage. Then you lead them to the pressroom in the back where they answer a few questions before returning to their seats."

241

"Sounds easy enough," Elizabeth said blandly.

*Leave it to Elizabeth,* Jessica thought dryly. *Thousands of girls would give their eyeteeth to do what Liz's doing, and she doesn't even care.*

"You'll have to leave two hours before Jess and I do, so they can show you around and get you dressed," Matt said.

*Dress!* Panic struck Jessica like a rocky avalanche. She'd been so enamored by the idea that she was Matt's date, she completely forgot she had nothing to wear to the awards ceremony. It figured; Jessica was about to go to the social event of a lifetime, and all she had to wear was a pair of grungy jeans and a T-shirt.

Matt motioned toward two *X*'s, side by side, in the second row of seats. "This is where we'll be," he said to Jessica.

Jessica smiled excitedly. "Do you know who we'll be sitting next to?"

"I have no idea, but you can bet they'll be rich and famous," Matt said with a smirk.

Jessica glowed. "This is too incredible."

Matt turned to Elizabeth. "What about Tom? When's he going to be there?"

"I'm not sure," Elizabeth answered, looking at her watch. "He probably just got back to campus an hour ago. Tonight he's going to dub as many videotapes of my statement as possible, and when he's done distributing them tomorrow, he'll drive back up here and meet me backstage."

"That's good," Matt said, nodding.

242

Elizabeth stood up and walked over to the phone. "In fact, I'll call him right now to see how everything's going."

Matt took Jessica by the hand. "Come on," he said. "I want to show you something."

Jessica followed him down the long hallway, her heart pounding fiercely in her chest. Matt's hand felt warm and strong in hers, yet tender at the same time. His profile was intense, as though he'd held on to some earth-shattering secret for years and was about to finally share it with someone else.

"What is it?" Jessica asked, fighting to keep her voice steady as she followed him into the master bedroom. The floor was covered in a thick silver carpet that sank underfoot. The furniture was sparse, but elegant, with the same lacquer and chrome motif as in the rest of the apartment. The king-sized bed was on a slightly higher level, with three carpeted stairs leading up to it. Recessed lights shone from underneath and around the perimeter of the bed, making it look as though it were floating on a cloud of light.

"Over here," Matt said, steering her to the walk-in closet.

Jessica's mouth gaped at the rows and rows of shoes, clothes, and coats. "This closet is bigger than my dorm room."

"It's too much, isn't it?" Matt flipped through the hangers. "I don't need all these clothes. I've decided that when this whole mess clears up, I'm giving most of it away to charity."

243

Jessica's fingers caressed a pair of black-and-white snake-skin boots. "It must be so nice to buy whatever you want," she said.

"It was fun at first, but then it got really boring. There was nothing to look forward to." Matt reached the end of the pole and started on the next wall. "Plus, the more stuff you own, the bigger the headaches. I think it's better to keep things simple."

"Thanks for the words of wisdom," Jessica answered as she scanned the rows of Italian suits. "But that's one lesson I'd like to learn on my own."

"Here it is," Matt said. He pulled a black garment bag off the rack and unzipped it.

Inside was the most exquisite formal gown Jessica had ever laid eyes on. It was long and sleek, with spaghetti straps and a slit from the bottom to mid-thigh. The color reminded Jessica of cotton candy. Tiny pink crystal-like beads were sewn onto the dress, shimmering under the light of the closet. It took her breath away.

"It's absolutely gorgeous," Jessica whispered. She reached out and gingerly touched the dress, the beads sparkling like diamonds.

Matt cleared his throat. "It was Julia's. She bought it when we were in Paris on vacation. It's an original by Jean-Marc Beauchamps."

Jessica pulled her hand away suddenly, as though it were too precious to touch. "She must've looked fabulous in this dress."

Matt's golden eyes were downcast. "Actually,

Julia never had a chance to wear it. She was saving it to wear to the Academy Awards if she were ever nominated for an Oscar."

*Life is so unfair,* Jessica thought sadly. *Julia had everything, but she didn't have enough time to enjoy it.*

"I was wondering if you'd do me a favor," Matt said, looking deeply into Jessica's eyes. "Would you wear this dress tomorrow night?"

Jessica felt as though the wind had just been knocked out of her. Julia Reynolds was a legend, and Jessica didn't think she could ever measure up. "I—I don't know," she stammered. "What if it doesn't fit?"

"We can have it altered," Matt implored. "Please, Jess. Wear it in her memory." He handed the dress to her.

Jessica draped the gown over her arm. She swallowed hard. A strange feeling of elation ballooned inside her, yet the heartbreaking circumstances of Julia's death were like a weighted string, keeping her anchored safely to earth. It was a dream come true for Jessica, but at the heavy cost of someone else.

"Of course I'll wear it," she said with a reserved smile. "I'll wear it for Julia."

"Everything you need is in here," Ronald Bishop said, handing a paper bag to Pierce. "Backstage pass, uniform—everything. You'll be posing as a cameraman at the ceremony."

"Perfect," Pierce answered, grabbing the bag

without hesitation. "Good work, Ronald."

Bishop was amazed at how much Pierce had changed in the past few weeks. Any trace of the shyness and timidity he'd once had was completely gone. Now he stood at his full height, making him several inches taller than Bishop. And instead of looking down at the floor, he stared straight ahead. His gaze was arrogant and hard.

Bishop looked away. "Did McKenna fill you in on the rest?"

"No, but I can figure it out for myself," Pierce snapped as he rifled through the bag. He stopped suddenly. "How am I supposed to arrive at the auditorium tomorrow night?"

Hot blood rushed to Bishop's face. He turned the air conditioner on high. "You have a car, don't you?"

Pierce snickered, as though the question were entirely absurd. "Sure, I have a car," he answered snidely. "You don't expect me to drive that old beat-up thing over there, do you?"

"Of course not," Bishop grumbled, wiping his forehead with a handkerchief. "I'll call for a car service to pick you up here."

Pierce gave Bishop a slap on the shoulder. "Don't forget to make it a round-trip," he said pointedly. "Actually, I might want to check out one or two of the celebrity bashes, so you'd better rent the car for the whole night."

Bishop's eyebrows narrowed. If Pierce thought he could lead him around like a puppy on a leash, he had news for him. "Do you think it's wise to be hanging around after you shoot Philip Markham?"

"I don't see why not," Pierce answered casually. "I have a feeling I'll want to celebrate. After all, I'll be coming into a great deal of money."

"You might be recognized."

Pierce grinned. "That scares you, doesn't it? Well, don't fret, Ronald. I'll take care to disguise myself." He pursed his lips thoughtfully. "But just to be on the safe side, maybe you should advance me a little cash so I can buy some fancy duds to change into."

Bishop pulled a wad of bills from his pocket and slipped off the money clip. "This should cover it," he said, gruffly handing over the money. "Is there anything else I can do for you?"

Pierce shoved the money in his pocket and gathered his things. "Nothing right now," he answered. "Just be sure to have the rest of the money waiting for me tomorrow night."

Bishop waved a thick finger at Pierce. "The money will be ready only if you kill Philip Markham."

"Don't worry about that, Ronny. I've been going to target practice." Pierce walked out of the office.

Bishop waited until he'd heard the door close before he picked up the phone. *This greedy kid isn't going to wreck everything I've worked for,* he mumbled to himself.

"Hello?"

"McKenna, this is Bishop. The kid's bleeding me dry. I think we need to go ahead with what we talked about," he said in a confidential tone. "As soon as Markham's dead, we'll take Pierce out of the picture, too."

"Are you nervous?"

Jessica's stomach turned a violent somersault. Here she was, in the backseat of a stretch limo, on her way to the Academy Awards with one of the most gorgeous actors on the planet, to stop an assassin. Why would she be nervous?

Jessica turned to Matt and smiled coyly. "Of course not," she answered.

"That's good," Matt said with a crooked smile. "I'm glad one of us isn't."

While Matt stared out through the tinted glass, Jessica's eyes were fixed on him. He was the most stunning man she'd ever seen. In his black European suit with satin lapels and white tuxedo shirt without a tie, Matt was completely devastating. The strong, sensuous curve of his mouth and jaw; the way his olive complexion played off his amber eyes and glossy hair; the way he carried his tall, well-defined frame. All of these things filled Jessica with an ache that worked its way deep into her bones. Matt was a perfect, priceless jewel, locked away behind a glass wall far beyond Jessica's reach. And Julia was the only one who'd held the key.

"You look great in that dress," Matt said, with a vague, distant smile.

Jessica ran her hand along the front of the gown, feeling the cool, slinky beads beneath her touch. "I can't believe it was a perfect fit."

Matt stroked Jessica's hand with his fingertips. He squinted at her, as though he were searching for something to say. "I'm glad I met you, Jess," he said hoarsely. "It's been hard . . . but you're so full of life. . . . You've made it bearable." He looked down shyly. "I want to thank you."

Then, as if in slow motion, he leaned toward her. The tip of his finger grazed Jessica's chin, carefully turning her face toward his. Matt's head tilted slightly to the side as he moved closer. Waiting for Matt's kiss, Jessica closed her eyes in ecstasy.

The instant his perfect mouth pressed against hers, Jessica felt as though she were bathing in a tranquil pool of cool light. His lips were feathery and soft as they traveled from her mouth to her cheek, lingering for one rapturous moment.

Then the limo came to a halt. The chauffeur lowered the glass partition between the driver's section and the backseat.

"We're here, Mr. Barron," he said. "Whenever you're ready."

Jessica had never seen so many people in one place. Thousands of screaming fans were on either side of them as they walked down the long red-carpeted path to the Shrine Auditorium. Arms waved, bulbs flashed, people pushed one another to get a better look at the next celebrity coming down the path. They flattened themselves against the police barricade, like angry bulls trying to break out of a pen.

*Only two weeks ago I was just like them,* Jessica thought with intense pleasure. *And now I'm at the Academy Awards.* She gave Matt's hand a squeeze. The memory of his kiss still tingled on her lips and cheek.

"How are you doing?" Matt asked, whispering in her ear. He waved, and the crowd roared.

"I'm fine," she said, watching the chaotic activity buzzing around her. "This is quite a trip."

A reporter up ahead spotted Matt and ran down the path to meet him. The sudden action set the whole group of reporters in motion, descending upon Matt and Jessica like a school of piranhas.

"Brace yourself, Jess, they're coming in for the kill," Matt warned. "You don't have to say a thing if you don't want to—just nod and smile a lot."

"Mr. Barron! Mr. Barron!" A reporter in an ill-fitting tuxedo nearly threw himself at their feet. "I understand you're accepting an award for Julia tonight," he said, thrusting a microphone in Matt's direction.

Matt flashed the television camera a blindingly charming smile. "I am. And I'm extremely honored to do so."

The reporter gave Jessica a smarmy smile. "And who's this delightful young woman?"

Jessica giggled airily as she inched her way from the slimy creature.

"She's my stylist," Matt said brightly.

Jessica nodded and gave Matt's arm a tug.

"Thank you for your time," Matt said as he followed Jessica down the red path. The crowd of reporters dissipated quickly as they spotted the next limo pulling up.

"You handled that very well," Jessica said, waving to the crowd like a queen appearing before her subjects. They looked at her with interest and awe. *I could get used to this,* she thought to herself.

"It's all part of the job," Matt said through smiling teeth. "You'll know all about it someday."

"Jessica!" a voice called from the side.

*Who would know me here?* she wondered, searching to find a face that matched the voice.

"Over here!"

Her eyes followed the sound and rested on a middle-aged man in a tuxedo. It was Don, the man who'd helped her on the movie set.

"Do you know that guy?" Matt asked, sounding edgy.

Jessica nodded and waved. "He helped me out when I was in a pinch." Don walked over to where they were standing. "What are you doing here?" she asked cheerfully.

"I'm working security tonight," Don answered. "Look at you—one week you've got a walk-on part, the next, you're going to the Oscars! That's one fast career."

251

Jessica introduced Matt to Don, and the two shook hands. "Some career . . . I got kicked off the set."

"That wasn't your fault." Don's voice suddenly dropped in volume. "Between you and me, Candice had a lot of problems. But don't let her get you down, kid. You've got a lot of talent."

"Do you think so?" Jessica asked, toying absently with the ends of her hair.

"There's no question," Don said, shaking his head. "I've seen many actors in my day, but you're a natural." .

Matt pointed to the entrance, where the ushers were motioning for the actors to enter the auditorium. "I think we'd better go," Matt said. He turned to Don. "It was nice meeting you."

"Likewise," Don answered. "Take care of yourself, Jessica. I'm sure we'll meet again."

"Thanks." Jessica beamed. Holding her head high and lifting the hem of her dress off the ground, she glided down the walkway with complete confidence, ready to take Hollywood by storm.

"Next!" the backstage security guard shouted.

Pierce stepped forward in line, his security pass dangling from a cord around his neck. The gun was in a leather holster strapped around his ankle. He tried to walk casually, even though every movement made him acutely aware of the weapon.

"Name, please," the security guard demanded.

Pierce held up the pass for him to read. The

guard eyed him curiously, then scanned down a list.

"What are you here for?" the guard demanded.

"I'm a cameraman," Pierce said dully.

The guard stared long and hard at him. Pierce met his gaze, amplifying the intensity until the guard broke down and looked away.

"Stand with your feet apart, arms out to the side," the guard ordered as he took out a black flattened baton. "Are you carrying a weapon, sir?"

"No." Pierce's heart slammed against his rib cage. He couldn't get caught now, not when he was so close to getting everything he'd ever wanted.

The guard turned on the metal detector, running it down along Pierce's arms and around his torso. Then he moved it to the inside of Pierce's legs. Pierce waited for the alarm to sound, but the detector remained quiet. The guard traveled down as far as Pierce's knees, then stopped.

"You can go," he said gruffly. "Next!"

Pierce dropped his hands against his sides and continued on toward the backstage area. The gun's handle scraped against his ankle with each step, rubbing his skin raw.

"Dancers for the opening number over here!" someone shouted. A group of people dressed in glittering leotards and gold body paint scurried over to the corner.

Pierce pushed on through the maze of people. Actors in formal wear, reporters in suits, production crew in jeans and sweatshirts—the place was a

253

motley collection of personalities and technical direction. Pierce walked around the roped-off press area and headed straight for the stage.

*Where's my target?* he wondered as he peered from the side of the stage out into the audience. The balcony was already filled with hyperactive fans, while the red VIP seats remained mostly empty. Philip Markham was supposed to win the Best Supporting Actor Oscar, so his seat was probably close to the front. Pierce's cold eyes scanned the rows, one at a time, until finally they stopped dead center.

He'd found his target.

The distinguished Philip Markham was in the front row. He looked around nervously, as though he were expecting something terrible to happen at any moment. A beautiful redhead who looked to be in her mid-thirties was sitting next to him, talking up a storm and touching his arm every few seconds. The sight of her annoyed Pierce, and he had a strange feeling that if he should miss Markham and hit her instead, it wouldn't be a tragic loss.

Pierce backed away from the stage and headed toward the dressing room. He stepped over thick bunches of cable and weaved through a graveyard of props. He had to find the perfect vantage point for his target. He had to get the perfect shot.

"Are you ready, Elizabeth?" Pierce heard a member of the staff say as one of the dressing room doors opened.

Pierce looked up. *How did she get here?* he wondered as he watched Elizabeth Wakefield walk out of the dressing room in a gold-sequined sheath. Pierce hid behind a painted backdrop of the Hollywood hills. Suddenly, he felt as if his plan were beginning to unravel like an old piece of rope.

Elizabeth sighed. She sounded nervous. "What do I need to do?"

"You'll be escorting the actors offstage to the press area," the staff member said. "As soon as they're done giving their acceptance speeches, come out, take them by the arm, and lead them away."

Pierce smiled to himself. Two targets standing in one delicious spot. It was almost too good to believe. *Why stop there?* he thought evilly. *Maybe I'll just try to wipe out as many people as I can.*

"Do you think you can do that?" the staff member asked.

Elizabeth nodded. "Yeah, I think so."

Suddenly, someone tapped Pierce on the shoulder. Startled, Pierce jumped back. "What?" he asked with agitation.

It was a man with a headset. "Are you going to hide behind the backdrop all night, or are you going to work the camera?"

Pierce laughed. *The camera.* He'd almost forgotten. "Where do I need to be?" he asked.

"Camera two." The man pointed to the camera situated in front of the stage.

*Dead center.*

"Perfect," Pierce said with a smile. "I'll be there all night."

255

# Chapter
## Seventeen

*Oh, wow, there's another one.*

Every time Jessica turned her head a fraction of an inch, she came face-to-face with another mega-star. They were all here: veteran actors, romantic leads, comedy kings—even a few musicians and models. It was odd to see so many recognizable faces around her. Somehow, Jessica expected them to look different close-up, but most of them looked pretty much the same as they did onscreen. But at the same time, they looked completely normal, like people she encountered in everyday life. Still, there was an aura of greatness in the room, a thriving energy of talent and achievement. Jessica was totally inspired.

"It's almost time," Matt said shakily.

Jessica patted his arm with reassurance. "Do you have your speech?"

Matt pushed his glossy hair away from his face.

"I didn't prepare one. I thought I'd just say whatever came to mind."

The audience applauded as the dancers left the stage and the emcee returned to the podium. The houselights dimmed, and the spotlight lit the stage.

"Tonight, we are here to honor the art of filmmaking and the many talented individuals who work tirelessly to perfect their craft," the emcee's voice boomed through the sound system. "But one person in particular, who devoted her life to acting, cannot be with us this evening. . . ."

Jessica heard a strange, rasping noise coming from Matt's direction. His face was pale and sweaty, and his fingers clutched at his throat. "Matt, are you all right?" she asked in panic.

"I can't do this," he wheezed. "I have to get out of here."

A photograph of Julia was projected on the large screen at the back of the stage.

"Julia Reynolds was a gifted and versatile actress who, in her short lifetime, starred in over thirty movies. Her roles ranged from the wacky older sister Maeve in *Surf Colony III*, to the sophisticated but sensitive socialite in *Debutante's Day Out*. . . ."

"Take a slow, deep breath," Jessica coached. "Just relax."

Matt obeyed, the color slowly returning to his face.

"This is Julia's big night," Jessica said soothingly. "You have to do this for her."

"I know," Matt whispered. His breathing became more even and steady. "I just panicked."

Jessica straightened Matt's jacket and smoothed back his hair. "She's with us tonight, you know. I can feel her here," Jessica said. "When you're up there accepting the award for her, she'll be standing right there with you."

Matt nodded and stared straight ahead.

"Tonight, we honor her memory and her work," the emcee continued. "And we thank Julia for adding a little something to each of our lives."

"That's your cue," Jessica whispered. She gave Matt a quick kiss on the cheek and nudged him toward the aisle.

Matt tentatively climbed the steps to the glass podium. The emcee handed Matt a gleaming Oscar and gave him a sympathetic hug. Matt looked at the shining statuette for several long moments, as if he were moved beyond words.

Tears rolled down Jessica's cheeks.

Finally, he spoke. "When I first met Julia, she was a young, talented, aspiring actress, with visions of making it in Hollywood. She knew the odds were against her. She'd seen too many of her friends' dreams go down the drain in their quest for fame. Still, she held the dream close to her heart and refused to give up. . . ."

Jessica wiped her eyes. Her chest felt heavy, as though a solid weight was pressing down on her.

"Soon, her first movie role came. It was for a film called *Open Road*. While the movie didn't do very well, it launched Julia into her next role, in the movie *Sociopath*. Suddenly, her career took off. . . ."

The pain Matt had been carrying inside seemed to pour out of him freely, on display for everyone to see.

"But what I loved best about Julia was that even when she became famous, she never changed. She was still the same sweet, down-to-earth girl I'd met fresh out of college. She was the most genuine person I have ever known . . ."

Matt's voice faltered, and a hush fell over the crowd. Jessica looked around. People were sniffling and dabbing their eyes. Everyone seemed to be moved.

He held up the statuette. "This was Julia's dream. Thank you for giving her the honor." Then he paused and looked toward the ceiling. "Wherever you are, Julia, I want you to know how much I love you."

The crowd sprung to its feet and exploded in thunderous applause. Jessica clapped the hardest, tears streaming down her face.

Elizabeth strolled onto the stage and looped her arm in Matt's, leading him to the pressroom. The audience sat back down, and the emcee took the mike once again.

"It's now my honor to present the nominees for Best Supporting Actor."

Jessica applauded once more, though keeping her eyes glued to the side doors, where she watched for Matt to reenter the theater. She couldn't wait to give him a hug, to tell him what a wonderful job he had done. Julia would've been proud.

"The nominees are, Walter Pettigrew for *My Daughter George* . . . Mason Avery Thomas for *A Weekend in Cleveland* . . . Jake Scovell for *Carnivore II—Medium Rare* . . . and Philip Markham for *Undesirable Starts with U*."

Jessica froze. *Philip Markham?* Jessica had been so busy basking in all the fame and wealth around her that she'd all but forgotten about Philip. The emcee was about to announce the winner, but neither Elizabeth nor Matt was anywhere in sight.

Hot liquid panic surged through Jessica's body. Any moment now, Philip would be taking the stage and someone, somewhere, would make an attempt on his life.

*Hurry, Matt,* Jessica pleaded silently. She had no idea what to do out here in the audience, all by herself. At the most crucial moment, their plan was quickly falling apart. *We can't mess up now,* Jessica thought tensely. One small mistake, and Philip Markham would be dead.

The emcee broke the gold seal and opened the envelope. "And the winner is . . ."

"That was a beautiful speech," Elizabeth said, leading Matt to the roped-off press area. She gave him a congratulatory peck on the cheek. "You did a good thing."

Matt exhaled. "It was so hard being up there. I kept thinking everyone was silently blaming me for Julia's death."

"That's not true," Elizabeth reassured him. "A lot of people sympathize with what you're going through," she said. "Besides, as soon as we catch the killer, your name will be cleared."

Matt looked at the swarm of reporters waiting to ask him questions. "I guess I'd better get this over with so we'll be ready when Philip takes the stage."

"I'll be waiting in the wings," Elizabeth said. "Good luck."

"Same to you. And be careful." Matt went off to the press area.

Elizabeth smoothed down her gold gown and trudged back to the side of the stage. The three-inch heels they had made her wear were giving her blisters, and the stage lights were as hot as a broiler oven. *I can't wait for this night to be over.*

"It's such an honor to be nominated with so many fine actors, I feel truly blessed . . ." A voice echoed from the podium.

*Yeah, yeah, we've heard it all before,* Elizabeth thought cynically. She'd been listening to acceptance speeches for the past two and a half hours, and every actor had the same spiel. It was as if none of them had an original thought. *Maybe they're so used to reading what they have to say, they can't come up with anything on their own.*

"I'd like to thank my parents, my wife and

four lovely children, everyone who's ever believed in me . . ."

Elizabeth curbed the urge to stick out her tongue and make gagging noises. *This guy's really laying it on thick.* Curiosity eventually got the best of her, and she peeked through the stage curtain to see who was speaking this time.

Elizabeth gasped. *It's Philip Markham!* Why didn't she realize he'd be next? She'd been wasting time while he was onstage, a perfect target for the assassin. In panic, she cowered away from the curtain.

*Hurry, Matt.* She tapped her foot anxiously, looking back at the press area. Reporters were swarming him; there was no way he'd even hear her if she called to him. Tom still hadn't shown up yet, and Jessica was out there in the audience by herself. The plans they'd discussed were disintegrating rapidly, like a pile of dead leaves in a brushfire.

". . . the members of the Academy, and most of all, I'd like to thank the fans."

Elizabeth pulled back the curtain, her eyes darting around the crowd. Nothing had happened yet, giving her the feeling that whoever was supposed to carry out the shooting was going to wait until Philip's speech was over. The actor was starting to wind things up, and judging from all the speeches before his, there was at least another minute to go.

*I don't see anything weird,* she thought as she

looked out at the crowd. A few people were listening attentively, others started to doze. Yet everyone seemed to be firmly grounded in their seats. There were no quick or unusual movements anywhere. She looked up at the lighting crew above. Everything seemed normal.

"Once again, thank you all for this great honor. I will treasure it forever."

*End of speech.* The audience applauded loudly. Elizabeth strode out onto the stage, suddenly feeling very vulnerable under the hot lights. All she had to do was lead Philip backstage, explain to him the situation, and try to convince him to sneak out the back exit.

"Congratulations, sir," she said, graciously taking his arm. "Right this way."

As they turned toward the stage exit, a sudden movement toward the front of the stage caught her eye. She looked back and saw the cameraman step out from behind the equipment and walk along the side of the stage. Instantly, she knew it was him. The assassin reached down and drew a gun. Without thinking, Elizabeth shielded Philip protectively and stared in horror as the assassin took aim.

Jessica's heart stopped as she watched the horrific event unfolding before her. Elizabeth had obviously spotted someone close to the stage, but too many heads blocked the view for her to see what was actually going on. The look of terror on

Elizabeth's face was enough for Jessica to know that her sister's life was in danger.

*Matt, where are you?* She looked toward the side of the stage, but no one was in sight. A murmur rippled through the crowd.

Suddenly, Elizabeth pushed Philip away and ran off the stage, leaping onto the steps in front. Jessica stood on her chair to get a better look at what was happening.

"What's going on here?" a voice called from out back.

"I think you'd better call the security guards," another one said to an usher.

From where she was standing, Jessica saw her sister wrestling the cameraman, her arms wrapped around his neck in a choke hold. His arms were flailing helplessly as he twirled around to throw Elizabeth off his back.

"That woman is attacking the cameraman!" somebody shouted. A few people in the front row gathered around them, when suddenly they both fell to the floor.

*What should I do?* Jessica thought weakly. This was nothing like what they had planned.

Philip Markham ran off the stage.

"Where's security?" the person in front of Jessica yelled.

Then suddenly a shot rang out.

The bullet sliced through the cable that suspended the stage lights overhead, sending the entire bank hurling toward the stage. It sputtered and fizzled, giving off sparks.

The room was chaos. "She's got a gun!" someone yelled, sending up cries of horror from the crowd. People either dove underneath their seats or ran for the back exits, dodging for cover.

"Elizabeth!" Jessica screamed, running for the stage. Guards rushed in from either side. A group of people stood around, watching the scuffle. Jessica shoved her way through. She had to see if Elizabeth was all right.

"We have the perpetrator," someone said to one of the guards.

Elbowing her way to the center of the crowd, Jessica looked to see a man holding Elizabeth with her hands behind her back. The man Elizabeth had been fighting was nowhere in sight.

"It's not her—she's innocent!" Jessica cried out. They looked at her as if she'd just announced that the world was flat. Up on the stage was the cameraman, hurrying toward the curtain. Jessica pointed furiously at him. "*He* has the gun!"

No one moved. The assassin disappeared behind the curtain. Elizabeth tried to wrestle free from the man's grip, when a police officer stepped forward and put the cuffs on her.

"You can't do this!" Jessica shouted at him. Elizabeth said nothing, but Jessica could feel her sister's fear. "You're letting the real killer get away!"

"Take her in," the police chief said to one of the officers.

Jessica followed alongside Elizabeth as they hauled her up the stage steps. "They can't do this to you, Liz," Jessica cried. "I won't let them."

Elizabeth looked at her with pleading eyes. "Don't leave me, Jess."

"I won't—I promise."

They walked through the curtain. Reaching the backstage area, Jessica saw Matt by the door. He had the assassin pinned to the ground.

Matt looked questioningly at Elizabeth, then at Jessica. "He was holding this," Matt said to the officer, handing over the gun.

The police chief raised his eyebrows, as he looked at the weapon. "Cuff him. I'll call for another squad car," he said to the officer. "We'll take them *both* in."

# Chapter
# Eighteen

_____

"We'll get you out of here as soon as we can," Jessica promised, putting her hands through the bars of the jail cell. "Matt's calling his lawyer right now."

Elizabeth squeezed her twin's hands, afraid to let go. She felt absolutely ridiculous in the dark, dingy holding cell, wearing a gold-sequined gown and high heels. Three tough-looking women were leaning against the far wall, smirking at Elizabeth.

"I heard them talking," Elizabeth whispered, pressing her cheek against the bars. "They think I'm the woman who's been stalking Philip. They think I had the gun."

Jessica shook her head. "That's crazy—you didn't even touch the gun."

"It doesn't matter what really happened," Elizabeth said in a shaky voice. Goose bumps prickled her skin. "They've already made up their minds."

Jessica lowered her head. "Bail won't be a problem. Matt said he'd cover everything."

Elizabeth swallowed hard. "I hope so," she said, looking over her shoulder. "I couldn't last the night in here." She leaned toward Jessica. "I think they know I'm innocent. I'll bet you anything the police chief here is one of Bishop's men, just like in Sweet Valley."

Jessica started to cry. "What are we going to do?"

The heavy steel door at the entrance of the corridor swung open, and a guard walked in. Elizabeth looked up to see Tom following behind. His dark eyes were sick with worry.

"You've got enough people here for a party, blondie," one of the women in the cell said.

Elizabeth shrugged off the comment, her fingers reaching out to touch Tom. "I'm so glad you made it," she said, her voice thick with emotion.

Tom pressed his face against the bars and gave Elizabeth a tender kiss. "I'm sorry I'm so late. The tapes took longer than I thought."

"Did you get them passed out?"

Tom nodded. "I brought Nina with me. She's waiting outside. We handed the tapes to every reporter at the Academy Awards."

"I hope they take it seriously," Jessica said.

Elizabeth held on tightly to both of them. "I just want this whole nightmare to end," she said.

The door squeaked open again, and the guard tapped Tom on the shoulder. "Visiting time is up," he said sternly.

Tom kissed Elizabeth again. The women in the cell whistled and cheered. "Get one for me," one of them said.

Tears dampened her eyes. "I wish you didn't have to go. . . ."

Jessica turned to the guard. "Put me in there with her."

"I can't do that," the guard answered. "Besides, she's not staying in the cell. I've been ordered to take her out for questioning."

"Tell them the whole story," Tom urged. "Don't let them intimidate you. We'll be waiting for you outside."

"We won't be far," Jessica added.

Elizabeth waved good-bye, blowing them a kiss as the guard hustled them out the door. A moment later, he came back and unlocked the cell.

"Okay, little lady, it's your turn," he said, swinging open the cell door. "There's someone who'd like to see you."

The door slammed shut, echoing off the solid-white walls. There were two folding chairs in the room, and Elizabeth sat in one of them, drumming her fingers nervously against the top of the smooth white folding table. There were no windows. The only thing of interest in the room was a television set built into the wall, but the control panel was covered by a lock.

*This is insane,* she thought to herself. From the moment she'd sensed she was in danger, Elizabeth had been running. She'd built a fortress inside herself to protect her sanity. Each setback in discovering the murderer had been like the sharp blow of a hammer, pounding away against her resolve. Every day in hiding had threatened the wall she'd built. And now, landing in jail was the final, crushing strike. All that was left was a pile of rubble strewn about her, leaving Elizabeth feeling exhausted and defenseless.

The door opened. Elizabeth didn't bother to look up. The sound of shoes clicking against the cement floor bounced off the walls.

"Elizabeth, it's nice to see you again."

Lifting her head, Elizabeth's eyes suddenly widened. "Detective Curtis—" She stopped for a moment, too stunned to speak. "How did you—"

The detective set his briefcase on the table. "I'm sorry they put you in here. You don't belong here." He patted her lightly on the back of the hand. "But I'm here to make sure they let you out."

Tears of relief streaked down her cheeks. "How did you know I was here? I thought you were in Hawaii."

"I was," the detective answered. "The day after I interviewed you about the fire, I left for vacation. But to tell you the truth, the whole situation bothered me. The bombing, and then the fact that some stranger had posed as an officer to question you. I had a feeling a case like that would just fall by the wayside in the department. My conscience wouldn't let me leave without checking into it a little further."

"So that's why you contacted Agent Leary."

Detective Curtis nodded somberly. "I was shocked to hear about Leary's murder," he said. "It really tipped me off that something was wrong. I contacted a few other agents and cut my vacation short."

Elizabeth sighed. Her body felt heavy, as though she were wearing a lead suit. "Thank you," she said. "I didn't think anyone was on my side."

"To tell you the truth, very few people were," the detective said frankly. "During the investigation, we discovered a lot of corruption within the department. Your suicide paper threatened to expose all of that." A grave expression darkened his features. "We were working as hard as we could to crack the case, but I was so afraid they'd get to you before we could. How did you manage?"

Elizabeth shrugged. She hadn't had any time to think about it. If she had, she probably would've fallen apart. "Just survival, I guess," she answered softly.

"You really should be proud of yourself. You did a great thing," Detective Curtis said with a smile. "At this very moment, your videotape is being played on every major television station in the country."

Elizabeth smiled weakly, then suddenly her face fell. "What happened with the guy who was after me?"

"He's being held for further questioning."

Elizabeth stood up. "I want to see him."

The detective's eyebrows narrowed. "Are you sure about that?"

"Absolutely," she said, walking toward the door. "Where is he?"

Elizabeth followed Detective Curtis out into the corridor to the second block of holding cells. She walked steadily, one foot in front of the other, her confidence building with each successive step. As the cell loomed closer, Elizabeth imagined a crumbling wall slowly reconstructing itself, bit by bit, like a film being played in reverse. She was strong again, her fortress restored to its original state.

"Detective Curtis—" An officer caught up with them, waving a stack of papers in the air. "I have it. We just got a full confession from him."

The detective clapped the officer on the shoulder. "Good work. Did he implicate everybody?"

"We think so," the officer answered. "The chief just sent a fleet of squad cars to make the arrests."

"Did you hear that, Elizabeth? Our man just squealed on everyone at Mammoth to get a reduced sentence," Curtis said. "He's still going away for a long time, though, with six counts of murder among other things." He reached for the handle of the door leading to the cellblock. "Are you sure you want to see him?"

Elizabeth nodded. The door swung open slowly, and Elizabeth was thankful to be watching it from the other side. The corridor was dark and smelled of mildew. She followed Curtis to the cell.

"Pierce, get over here!" Detective Curtis demanded.

A young man, sitting on the bunk against the wall, looked up. Elizabeth remembered the narrow face, the dark mustache. Somehow he looked much younger and much more helpless.

"I'll be right here, Elizabeth," Detective Curtis said, standing only a few feet away.

Pierce's head fell against his chest. He made no motion to get up from the bunk.

"Why did you do this to me?" Elizabeth asked, her voice steady. "Why did you want to make my life a living hell?"

Pierce slid off the bunk, his body as languid and spineless as a snake. He approached the bars, keeping himself at a distance. "I'm sorry," he said, his voice just above a whisper.

"You disgust me," Elizabeth said evenly. "You've ruined so many people's lives."

Pierce nodded almost imperceptibly, as though he agreed with every word.

A stream of insults and accusations waited on her tongue, ready to be hurled like bullets in Pierce's direction. But Elizabeth held back and swallowed them, instead. She wasn't quite sure what stopped her, whether it was the fact that he'd been a pawn in Ronald Bishop's game or if it was the lost, soulless look in Pierce's eyes. Somewhere along the line, the humanity had been drained from him, leaving only a dry, crumbling shell.

Elizabeth turned to Detective Curtis. "I've had enough," she said, turning away.

Opening the door, he led her down the hallway, toward the front offices. "You're a very brave young woman," he said, shaking her hand.

"Thank you for all your help," she said gratefully. "I thought this nightmare would never end."

"Well, it has," he said with a smile. "You're free to go."

Elizabeth walked out of the police station, daring to smile for the first time since the whole mess began. The sun warmed her skin as she descended the steps to the parking lot where everyone was waiting. She kicked off her gold pumps and did a little dance on the pavement. It felt good to be free.

"The woman of the hour!" Tom shouted. Matt and Jessica cheered.

Nina wrapped an arm around Elizabeth's shoulders. "I'm so glad you're all right. These past few weeks have been terrible without you. I've had absolutely no one to complain to."

Elizabeth gave Nina a big hug. "It's so great to see you," she said.

Jessica grabbed her sister's hand. "I just want you to know that I'm sorry I gave you such a hard time," she said apologetically. "You were brilliant, Liz."

Elizabeth blushed. "Was I really?"

Matt held out his hand. "I'll forever be in your debt. Thanks for everything."

Elizabeth looked deeply into his eyes, nodding. "You're welcome," she answered. She turned to Tom, a playful smile returning to her lips. "And what do *you* have to say for yourself?"

Tom curved his arm around her waist. "This—," he said, tipping her back in a graceful dip, then pulling her up to kiss her full on the lips.

Jessica rolled her eyes. "Let's get out of here before I gag."

Matt took Jessica by the hand and led her to his car. It suddenly occurred to her, now that the whole ordeal was becoming a part of their past, that Matt was more than just a movie star she'd had the good fortune to meet. He was a friend. They actually had a history together. Jessica had been there for him when Matt had been hanging by a thread, and he'd been there for her. All these things probably weren't enough to base a relationship on, but it was a good start.

"Thank you so much, Jessica," Matt said. Sadness seemed to linger in his golden eyes, although Jessica detected a faint glow, as if the slightest sliver of happiness had been restored to him.

"It was my pleasure," she said huskily. Now that the search for Julia's murderer was over, there was so much Jessica wanted to tell him. So much she wanted to share about her life. She didn't know where to begin. "What happens now?"

Matt looked down at the set of car keys in his hand. "I thought I'd go to Europe for a while . . ."

*By myself.* The words hung in the air, unspoken.

Jessica's heart felt like a ship's anchor, falling endlessly through colder and colder water, never reaching bottom. "That sounds great," she said meekly.

Matt touched her hand. "I really need to think, to sort things out."

"What about acting?" she asked, grasping for something to hold on to. "What about your career?"

Matt ran a hand through his hair. "I'm tired of the Hollywood scene. I just want to simplify my life. I don't know if I'll ever go back." His fingers traced the outline of her cheekbone. "But you should go ahead and follow your dream of acting. Do that for me."

"I will," Jessica promised. The warmth of his touch seemed to be melting into her skin. "I'm going to miss you."

Matt's thumb caressed the outline of her lips. Jessica held his gaze, afraid that if she even blinked, he'd disappear. His strong arms reached out and pulled her against him. Jessica's hands followed the contour of his collarbone, up and around, meeting at the warm spot at the back of his neck. With a graceful motion, Matt leaned over, tilted Jessica's head back, and pressed his soft mouth against hers.

Matt's lips brushed across Jessica's cheek up to her ear, sending chills through her. "Someday you'll meet someone who'll make you feel like a star."

276

Wordlessly, Jessica watched as Matt climbed into his black Ferrari, on his way to exotic locations, seeking adventures she'd never know about. But wherever life would take him, Jessica hoped he'd find true happiness.

Remembering what Matt had said, Jessica smiled. And as she watched him drive away, with the taste of his kiss still lingering on her lips, she knew in her heart that he was right. And that everything would be okay.

# SWEET VALLEY HIGH™

### Created by Francine Pascal

Why not backtrack and check-out what happened in Sweet Valley before university! The bestselling Sweet Valley High series are published by Bantam Books.

1. DOUBLE LOVE
2. SECRETS
3. PLAYING WITH FIRE
4. POWER PLAY
6. DANGEROUS LOVE
7. DEAR SISTER
8. HEARTBREAKER
9. RACING HEARTS
10. WRONG KIND OF GIRL
11. TOO GOOD TO BE TRUE
12. WHEN LOVE DIES
13. KIDNAPPED
14. DECEPTIONS
15. PROMISES
18. HEAD OVER HEELS
23. SAY GOODBYE
26. HOSTAGE
27. LOVESTRUCK
32. THE NEW JESSICA
35. OUT OF CONTROL
36. LAST CHANCE
44. PRETENCES

54. TWO-BOY WEEKEND
63. THE NEW ELIZABETH
67. THE PARENT PLOT
74. THE PERFECT GIRL
75. AMY'S TRUE LOVE
76. MISS TEEN SWEET VALLEY
77. CHEATING TO WIN
80. THE GIRL THEY BOTH LOVED
82. KIDNAPPED BY THE CULT!
83. STEVEN'S BRIDE
84. THE STOLEN DIARY
86. JESSICA AGAINSY BRUCE
87. MY BEST FRIEND'S BOYFRIEND
89. ELIZABETH BETRAYED
90. DON'T GO HOME WITH JOHN
91. IN LOVE WITH A PRINCE
92. SHE'S NOT WHAT SHE SEEMS
93. STEPSISTERS
94. ARE WE IN LOVE?

# SWEET VALLEY HIGH™

*Prom Thriller mini-series*
Thriller: A NIGHT TO REMEMBER
   95. THE MORNING AFTER
   97. THE VERDICT
   98. THE WEDDING
   99. BEWARE THE BABYSITTER
  100. THE EVIL TWIN

*Romance trilogy*
  101. THE BOYFRIEND WAR
  102. ALMOST MARRIED
  103. OPERATION LOVE MATCH

*Horror in London mini-series*
  104. LOVE AND DEATH IN
        LONDON
  105. A DATE WITH A WEREWOLF
  106. BEWARE THE WOLFMAN

*Love and Lies mini-series*
  107. JESSICA'S SECRET LOVE
  108. LEFT AT THE ALTAR!
  109. DOUBLECROSSED
  110. DEATH THREAT
  111. A DEADLY CHRISTMAS

*Winners and Losers mini-series*
  112. JESSICA QUITS THE SQUAD
  113. THE POM-POM WARS
  114. 'V' FOR VICTORY

*Desert Adventure mini-series*
  115. THE TREASURE OF DEATH
        VALLEY
  116. NIGHTMARE IN DEATH
        VALLEY

*Loving Ambitions mini-series*
  117. JESSICA THE GENIUS
  118. COLLEGE WEEKEND
  119. JESSICA'S OLDER GUY

*Rivalries mini-series*
  120. IN LOVE WITH THE ENEMY
  121. THE HIGH-SCHOOL WAR
  122. A KISS BEFORE DYING

*Camp Echo*
  123. ELIZABETH'S RIVALS
  124. MEET ME AT MIDNIGHT
  125. CAMP KILLER

*Thriller editions*
MURDER ON THE LINE
MURDER IN PARADISE

*Sweet Valley High Super Stars*
BRUCE'S STORY
ENID'S STORY
TODD'S STORY

*Super editions*
SPECIAL CHRISTMAS
PERFECT SUMMER
SPRING FEVER

*Special editions*
THE WAKEFIELDS OF SWEET
  VALLEY
THE WAKEFIELD LEGACY

# THE SADDLE CLUB

by Bonnie Bryant

Saddle up for another exciting ride with Stevie, Carole and Lisa. These three very different girls come together to share their special love of horses and to create The Saddle Club.

Ask your bookseller for any titles you may have missed. The Saddle Club series is published by Bantam Books.

1. HORSE CRAZY ✓
2. HORSE SHY
3. HORSE SENSE ✓
4. HORSE POWER ✓
5. TRAIL MATES ✓
6. DUDE RANCH ✓
7. HORSE PLAY
8. HORSE SHOW ✓
9. HOOF BEAT ✓
10. RIDING CAMP ✓
12. RODEO RIDER ✓
13. STARLIGHT CHRISTMAS ✓
14. SEA HORSE ✓
15. TEAM PLAY
16. HORSE GAMES
17. HORSENAPPED·
18. PACK TRIP
19. STAR RIDER
20. SNOW RIDE
21. RACE HORSE
22. FOX HUNT ✓
23. HORSE TROUBLE
24. GHOST RIDER
25. SHOW HORSE
26. BEACH RIDE
27. BRIDLE PATH
28. STABLE MANNERS

# THE SADDLE CLUB

by Bonnie Bryant

29. RANCH HANDS
30. AUTUMN TRAIL
31. HAY RIDE
32. CHOCOLATE HORSE
33. HIGH HORSE
34. HAY FEVER
35. HORSE TALE
36. RIDING LESSON
37. STAGE COACH
38. HORSE TRADE
39. PURE BRED
40. GIFT HORSE
41. STABLE WITCH
42. SADDLEBAGS
43. PHOTO FINISH
44. HORSE SHOE
45. STABLE GROOM
46. FLYING HORSE
47. HORSE MAGIC
48. MYSTERY RIDE
49. STABLE FAREWELL
50. YANKEE SWAP
51. PLEASURE HORSE
52. RIDING CLASS
53. HORSE SITTERS
54. GOLD MEDAL RIDER
55. GOLD MEDAL HORSE

*Super Editions*

1. A SUMMER WITHOUT HORSES
2. THE SECRET OF THE STALLION
3. WESTERN STAR
4. DREAM HORSE

We hope you enjoyed reading this book. If you would like to receive further information about available titles in the Bantam series, just write to the address below, with your name and address:

KIM PRIOR
Bantam Books
61–63 Uxbridge Road
London W5 5SA

If you live in Australia or New Zealand and would like more information about the series, please write to:

SALLY PORTER
Transworld Publishers (Australia) Pty Ltd
15–25 Helles Avenue
Moorebank
NSW 2170
AUSTRALIA

KIRI MARTIN
Transworld Publishers (NZ) Ltd
3 William Pickering Drive
Albany
Auckland
NEW ZEALAND

All Transworld titles are available by post from:
Book Service By Post, PO Box 29,
Douglas, Isle of Man IM99 1BQ

Credit cards accepted.
Please telephone 01624 675137, fax 01624 670923
or Internet htt://www.bookpost.co.uk for details

Please allow for post and packing:
UK: £0.75 per book
Overseas: £1.00 per book